COSTUME SHOP

By

Bobby Legend

COSTUME SHOP

Published through Legend Publishing Company
This is a work of fiction. Names, characters, places, and incidents are the product of the author's imagination or are used fictitiously.   Any resemblance to actual persons, living or dead, events, or locales is entirely coincidental.

Copyright © 2014 Bobby Legend (2017 2nd Edition)
Book Design and Layout by Mickey Strange
ISBN 978-0-9821687-6-9

INTRODUCTION

COSTUME SHOP

Watch your step when you enter this costume shop. You are stepping into the realm of science fiction. You may not like or understand what you see.

Detective Zoolu has his work cut out for him when his partner disappears and was last known to have visited some out of the way costume shop. But does this costume shop even exist? That's the predicament that Detective Zoolu must confront.

Other detectives were unable to find this mysterious costume shop…because there were no commercial road maps that showed the area in question. However, eyewitnesses, many of whom ended up in the mental institution, gave them the description of it and they still couldn't find it. But Zoolu did find the shop, and the weird town that surrounded it.

But where was Zoolu's partner? Did the hunchbacked, old man that ran this mysterious costume shop have something to do with his disappearance? Did the old man kill him and then bury him in the barren desert that surrounded this mysterious costume shop that supposedly, didn't exist?

Step inside this mysterious costume shop and try on your costume. That is, if you can find the place. Will you be one of the lucky ones to visit this shop…or one of the unlucky ones, when you visit this realm of science fiction?

CHAPTER 1

My name is Bobby Legend…and I'm an investigative reporter for an independent newspaper.

One morning, not too far back, I was awakened by a loud knock on my front door. But when I answered it there wasn't anyone around. However, the visitor did leave something for me to see: a small 9 by 12-inch catalog envelope that was attached to the doorknob – which I quickly retrieved and opened…and found that it contained a small handwritten journal. Glancing through it, I was happy to see that it had information concerning a story I was investigating…called "The Legend of Hollow Pass."

So, with journal in hand, I went back inside my abode to the living room, sat down on my couch and began reading the mysterious journal – not expecting too much to come out of it. But once I started reading it…I couldn't stop…and read it in one sitting, without any interruptions or breaks…because what this person had to say was very intriguing to say the least.

This is what the journal's author had to say: My name is Detective Brad Zoolu…and I've written this book in the hopes that someone will take on my quest for the truth behind the "Legend of Hollow Pass." That is, if for some reason I can't finish it myself. This is my story.

I had been working in the State police homicide department for over twenty-five years when my partner of twenty-three years, Charles Webber, suddenly disappeared. He had left for the weekend and was due back to work two days later but he never showed up. After searching – with no luck – every bar, saloon, and any other place where I thought he might be, I gave up…and began my investigation on his disappearance. The only lead I had to go on was a conversation my partner had had with me. He mentioned that he was going to check out a little, out-of-the-way costume shop off the main highway in a small town in the desert. He wanted to ask the shop owner a few questions concerning the disappearance of an ex-girlfriend, and also to ask about renting a costume for himself for the policeman's ball that was coming up in a few days. But it was a very strange conversation. When I told him there was no desert in this area, he suddenly clammed up…and refused to divulge any information until he was certain about the facts.

He mumbled something about the "Legend of Hollow Pass." I wasn't familiar with the legend, or the story behind it, so I didn't pay any attention to him. I figured it was just an old wives' tale. He also mentioned how he had found this strange town…and how it seemed to rise out of nowhere. When I questioned his sanity, he again maintained that the town had just suddenly appeared…and then refused to say any more about it. I was confused and concerned over his demeanor and the strange conversation that I had had with him. He had talked about a desert and mountainous area. But as far as I knew, there wasn't any desert or mountainous area in this region. That was one reason why our conversation had left me unsettled. He wanted to see if he could find the place again.

That was the last time I had seen or talked with him. So I tried to find this place on my own using the scant information obtained through our conversation. Even though I couldn't come up with a telephone number or address, I did find, however, a dirty piece of paper that had "Highway 5, and Costume Shop" written on it along with the name of a detective from the Department of Missing Persons, taped to the back of my partner's desk drawer, as if he had been trying to keep it hidden from prying eyes.

My partner, I was certain, had hidden this paper. The writing was faint and smudged so I couldn't read the complete name of the detective. And there were other words and sentences that were hard to read, too. But one of the words that I could read besides Highway 5 and Costume Shop was underlined. And that word was "*Legend*." I had absolutely no idea what my partner was trying to get at. But he had also drawn the mountain and canyon road leading to this costume shop. So I looked on our state maps but couldn't find this area anywhere. I even looked on our county road maps, but there wasn't anything that looked like the picture my partner had drawn. But that didn't faze me. I was going to find this place no matter what.

The very next morning, I jumped into my car and tried to find the costume shop my partner had mentioned. I had been driving forever, but I still couldn't find this place. Jeez, am I lost or what, I thought to myself. More than two and half-hours had passed as I tried to find some out-of-the-way costume shop that was supposedly in the middle of the desert. Only thing was...I couldn't find any desert ... Or mountains. So I decided to give up and return to the station empty-handed. I quickly made a U-turn and pushed the car's accelerator to the floor hoping to reach the station within four hours. During the ride, I thought about my missing partner.

Supposedly, he had been to the shop a year or so earlier when he had been on loan to the Department of Missing Persons and was searching for a lost maiden. He had given me a description of the area, and some crazy story, but at that time I wasn't interested. It wasn't my investigation, so I didn't really care one way or another.

Suddenly, my thoughts were interrupted when the main highway seemed to disappear in a flash and, out of nowhere, as if it were a mirage, a large, dark cloud enveloped my car. I soon found myself driving up a steep and high mountainous road; one similar to the description that my partner had given me. So I knew I was on the right track. But I couldn't see any desert!

As my car slowly climbed the very steep, mountainous road, the weather suddenly changed for the worse. A crisp and harsh wind began pounding and rocking my automobile as more and more clouds and a very thick and wet misty fog seemed to smother it, making it impossible to see. I now had almost zero visibility.

And then, for some unknown reason, my car slowed to a crawl, as though some strange power had taken over...and was controlling it. I prayed I was traveling in the right direction, towards my destination. I didn't really understand or know what the heck was going on, but I knew something wasn't right.

As the wind rocked and pounded my car, I continued my ascent up the winding, narrow mountainous road. And as I reached the top of this strange mountain, large pine trees growing on both sides of the road began slapping and pounding my car with their thick branches and leaves.

As I tried to race away, I suddenly lost control of my car. Something seemed to take over my mind and body, as my car seemed to maneuver without my guidance. It was as though I was paralyzed from the neck down. My body seemed to be glued to the seat – like a heavy, two-ton weight had been set upon my lap. I was helpless.

The wind pushed my car all over the dirt road as it traveled downward, picking up speed faster and faster, like a bat out of hell. I thought the car was going out of control and was going to crash and fall three thousand feet into the deep, dark ravine below.

But to my surprise, the car slowed to a crawl when it reached the bottom of the mountain. I was finally on the canyon floor. I regained control of my car and my senses, even though my mind was still somewhat clouded from the weird sensations I had experienced. I felt as though I had been drugged.

As I sat in my car on the canyon floor trying to regain my senses, a glimmer of sunshine suddenly came through the dark clouds and thick fog, shining its golden rays over a dirt road which seemed to point the way – to the place I had been searching for. I could now see a small town a few miles ahead. And it <u>was</u> in the middle of a desert!

I slowly pressed down on the car's accelerator and followed the dirt road, hoping it would lead me to the costume shop. As I drove slowly towards this strange, little town, I checked out the surrounding area. It was so bare and desolate that the only plant life around was tumbleweeds and cactus. This town was isolated from everything and everyone.

As I neared the town, there was nobody in sight. I thought it was a ghost town. It looked like it had been built back in the civil war days during a gold rush…and reminded me of an old mining town. Because many of the few buildings remaining on the only street in town were empty shells and barely able to stand. I guess you could call it Main Street.

After passing about six small, partially fallen and empty wooden buildings, I finally came to the last building – an old, rickety, dilapidated – but intact – wooden shack. Over the front door was a weathered sign – that looked as though it hadn't been painted in ten years – that read: "Costume Shop." Finally, I thought, this must be the costume shop I was looking for. So I parked my car in front of the shop and as I did, my investigative instincts kicked in. Even though my mind was still cloudy and confused from the ride I had just experienced, my investigative instincts were not. I was quite anxious to question the shop's occupants.

Stepping out of my vehicle, I instinctively glanced around the town and noticed a small, dirty, malnutrition boy staring at me as he tried to hide behind the side of one of the nearby buildings. He looked as though he hadn't bathed in years and was in need of a friend. So I smiled and waved at him while opening the front door of the costume shop. But the boy didn't react. I shrugged my shoulders and entered the little shop.

Closing the door behind me, I quickly glanced around the small, twelve-foot by twelve-foot room and noticed a partitioned corner cubicle used as a changing room and many rows of costumes, while four or five mannequins dressed in beautiful and very expensive, decorative outfits stood guard in different areas of the room.

Many of the store's costumes seemed to be handmade; there were hundreds of them – and all were masterpieces in design and craftsmanship and each one priceless. I was amazed to see such an array of costumes in such a small shop. And in the middle of the desert, no less: a desert I never knew existed.

Behind the only counter in the store – and the only other person in the store besides me – stood an old and small, hunchbacked man with a wrinkled face and a balding head, who wore thick-lensed, wire-rimmed eyeglasses that magnified his eyes ten times their normal size...which seemed to bulge out of his cherub-round face. He was dressed in a renaissance costume, and reminded me of a hunchbacked Ben Franklin. But this guy was no founding father. He was barely five-feet tall and must have weighed a good two hundred pounds. The blank stare from his protruding, buggy eyes followed me around the room, as I looked over the costumes and his shop.

"Can I help you?" asked the old man in a slow and deep southern drawl, as he cleaned and repaired a soldier's Civil War costume.

Just as I was about to speak, I began to choke and cough uncontrollably. Suddenly, I got a very bad taste in my mouth and a burning sensation deep inside my esophagus trailing down into my stomach. It was as if an acid bomb had exploded inside my body. Trying to catch my breath, I finally cleared my throat long enough to say a few words.

"Yeah. I'm Detective Brad Zoolu," I said, showing him my gold shield and police identification. "I would like to ask you a few questions concerning my partner's disappearance." With that said and staring straight into his eyes, I showed him a Polaroid picture of my partner, hoping to get some kind of reaction from him.

"Who is he?" he asked, peering over his thick-lensed glasses.

"He was a detective. And he was here investigating a missing person's case...and was going to rent a costume for the policeman's ball. Do you remember if he came into this shop to do that?"

After staring at the photo for nearly a minute, the old, decrepit man just shrugged his shoulders and said, "I don't remember him."

"Would you possibly have it in your records?" I asked him. "Any information you can give me would be of great help."

"I'm sorry, but my mind is a little slow at the moment. The picture really doesn't jog my memory. But if you leave your telephone number, I will go through my records and see if I have his receipt. If I do, I'll give you a call?"

"Fair enough. Before I leave, I'll give you my business card. That has my telephone number and address on it."

He looked at me and nodded, then went back to fiddling with a costume. As he worked, I walked around the small room, checking every nook and cranny, and periodically watched him as he cleaned the costume in his lap. It looked similar to the costume my partner had talked about renting. When he noticed I was staring at it, he nonchalantly stopped working on it and set it to the side out of sight. It seemed as if he was trying to hide it without me noticing what he was up to. And he was definitely trying to hide it! But why, I thought? Why would he want to conceal this particular costume? I decided it was just my imagination running wild and that my suspicious nature was getting the best of me. So I put the thought out of my mind…for the time being.

"Well, please give me a call if you remember anything. If I'm not in my office, you can leave a message and a number and I will return your call." Looking deep into his eyes, I added, "I'll be back anyway. I want to rent a costume for our policeman's ball."

"Fine. You can rent a costume anytime."

"I'm sorry, what is your name?"

"My name…is Jackson Billing," he said, peering over his thick glasses.

"Thank you for your time, Mr. Billing," I said, and then handed him my business card before leaving the shop.

I felt very lightheaded as I stepped out of that shop into the crisp desert air. But sobered up quickly when I noticed that filthy little boy staring at me again. This time he was hiding behind a large, dilapidated sign. He acted like a deaf-mute.

The costume shop owner and that little boy were the only two people I had seen in that town on that eerie day.

Suddenly, I became frightened as if I was a small child again, all alone in a ghost town. I quickly jumped into my car and sped away from that strange, deserted town. Within a few minutes I was well on my way and heading for home. A few miles later, I again began climbing the steep and winding mountain road, hoping it would lead me out of this eerie area and back to familiar surroundings.

And just as I was beginning to feel at ease, my mind suddenly became bogged down in a deep fog. I was in another deep trance. And my body had become paralyzed once again. I couldn't move a muscle. Something or someone else had taken control of my body…and car.

And the higher the car climbed up the mountainous road, the weather worsened. Mother Nature seemed to be enraged by my presence…because the wind began howling. And the blowing winds, roaring like a massive hurricane began rocking my car, while the dark clouds overhead began rolling by faster and faster as a thick fog surrounded the area. The same thing happened when I first entered this strange area. Now it was happening again, going back. What had I run into, I thought to myself? What devil lurks behind this area? I didn't want to know, but I had to find out what had happened to my partner.

After what seemed like an eternity, I was finally out of that ungodly area. The dark cloud that had smothered my car had evaporated within a nanosecond. The main road I had followed from my partner's faded words on that dirty piece of paper seemed to appear right in front of my eyes. When I looked into my rear-view mirror, the mountainous road suddenly vanished behind me as if it had been an illusion. My mind was very confused and clouded in mystery and disbelief. I wasn't sure what I had just experienced.

But questions abound. And I was anxious to get back to the station…to see if I could find any of my partner's case files. Especially the last one he had been investigating. I was hoping that it might help me answer some of the questions surrounding his disappearance and the strange area I had come across.

I returned to the station and sat down at my desk to think about my next step in this investigation. I really needed to find my partner's files. But when I checked his desk and locker, there wasn't a whole lot of evidence to be found. Other than a couple pages of scribbled notes, I didn't find anything else pertaining to my investigation. All I had were the few notes and faded words on that piece of paper that he had hidden and taped to the back of his desk drawer. I would look over the scribbled notes later, at my home, to see if I could get any leads.

My search of my partner's desk and locker had ended on a sour note. So I decided to head over to his apartment and search there for any evidence pertaining to his disappearance.

But during my drive to my partner's apartment, I kept thinking about that fat, little, old, hunchbacked man at the costume shop. My gut instinct told me that he was somehow linked to my partner's disappearance. But then my intellectual reasoning told me that he wasn't. My brain was on fire. I couldn't get my partner's disappearance out of my mind.

Once I had arrived at the apartment, I used my partner's extra key that was hidden under a flowerpot near the front door and let myself in. I searched his apartment very thoroughly, spending nearly five hours rifling through every dresser and desk drawer and every closet, but found nothing that would help me in my investigation. The only thing that caught my eye was a short note that was written by my partner and left on the kitchen table, reminding him to check out the costume shop. What was so important about that weird shop that he needed to write a note reminding himself about it? I was even more confused now, and left his apartment shaking my head in frustration.

Now I wanted to drive back home and look over my partner's scribbled notes to see if I could make some sense out of them. But first I had to get some rest. I had been up for over twenty-four hours already.

I needed to get a good night's sleep so I could get a fresh start in the morning. But once at home sleeping was difficult…because I kept waking up in a deep sweat from a horrifying nightmare about that little, hunchbacked fat man, who turned into the devil and inhaled my partner's body into his mouth…and within a few seconds had consumed him completely.

That's when I would wake up, my heart pounding five hundred beats per minute. Although I would fall back to sleep, the nightmare kept returning to haunt me. And each time…there would be a little more added to it. After he swallowed my partner, I could see his bulging, glaring eyes, magnified a hundred times, calling for me. And as I felt myself being pulled towards his repulsive body, I would awaken, my body completely drenched in sweat.

Finally, I couldn't take it anymore and decided to stay up. And when I looked over at my alarm clock to check the time, it was already five in the morning – time to rise and shine. But my body was very sluggish and tired. I felt as though I had gotten only twenty minutes of sleep, if that. And wondered if that strange weather had anything to do with my restless feelings.

Something was happening to my body and my mind, but I couldn't put my finger on it. However, once I had jumped into the shower and felt the warm water on my bare skin, the tension seemed to ease. So I showered that morning twice as long as usual, and it seemed to help soothe my strange feelings. Once my shower had ended, I quickly dried my body, dressed and ate a small continental breakfast. Now I was ready to return to the station.

I had many things to do. And the first thing was to ask the detective in the Missing Person's Department a few questions. I hoped he could give me a little insight into my partner's whereabouts. Even though I couldn't completely make out the detective's full name on my partner's dirty piece of paper, I was sure I knew who the person was he had written about. And the only way I would know for certain would be to ask that person myself.

CHAPTER 2

While driving to the station, thinking about that costume shop completely consumed my mind. So much so that I couldn't even remember what streets I had driven on to get there. I figured I was just overly tired. Once I had reached my desk, I finally felt at ease. But before I did anything, I needed a cup of hot, black coffee to wake me up; after that, I would be ready for anything…and roaring and ready to go.

After visiting the station's snack bar and drinking the much-needed nectar of energy, I returned to my desk, sat back in my chair and began pouring over the scribbled notes. There wasn't much to go through, but any information would be helpful. Some of the important words were underlined – like <u>Talk to boy</u> and <u>Waters</u>, which I understood to be the name of the detective in the Missing Person's Department. It was also the same word that had been written on the faded and smudged piece of paper.

I was sure that my partner meant Detective Waters. And he was the next person I wanted to question. I was hoping he might be able to shed some light on my partner's disappearance and fill in some of the missing pieces to the puzzle. I wasn't going to leave any stone unturned in my search for the truth.

I also wanted to search for my partner's missing case files again. I knew they had to be around the office somewhere…and that I had just overlooked them. But I would do that a little later…right after I had my little talk with Detective Waters.

After drinking another cup of coffee, I was ready to visit him. So I walked downstairs to the Missing Person's Department and to his desk…where he was reading the newspaper. When he noticed me, he quickly folded up his paper and set it on the floor beside him.

"What can I do for you, Zoolu?" he asked.

Standing in front of his desk, I replied, "Hello Detective Waters. I need to speak with you about a little, hunchbacked, old man who owns a costume shop in the desert. I think he is somehow involved in my partner's disappearance. Do you know anything about this guy and his costume shop?"

He nodded. "I might be able to help you. Although I don't know a hell of a lot."

I pulled up a chair and sat in it, telling him, "Something just doesn't feel right to me. I'd bet money that that old man is involved with my partner's disappearance."

"That hunchbacked old man is a strange case…that's for sure. But I could never find any evidence against him concerning my investigation. A lot of conjecture, circumstance, and rumor…but no hard evidence."

"I don't like anything about that crazy place," I added.

"I didn't like anything about that place. Or the case I was investigating. That was nearly two years ago and I still haven't gotten it out of my mind. There were many strange happenings going on out there."

"I experienced some mighty strange phenomenon, too. What did you experience?"

Waters lit a cigarette, took a long drag, exhaled the smoke, and then said, "All I remember about the drive there…was the howling, blowing wind and foul weather that nearly blew my car off the road and into the ravine, two thousand feet below. It was nerve racking to say the least."

"Same here," I replied. "I have never experienced anything like that in my life. That place seemed to just appear out of the clouds. What gives?"

"You tell me! When I checked our official local maps, I couldn't find that town anywhere. And it's all mountainous area! But yet that town is in the middle of a desert. To this day, I still don't remember how I even got there."

"You had that trouble too, huh?"

But instead of answering my question, he gave me a dirty look, saying, "Listen, I don't want to talk too much about my little episode. People around here tend to have big ears and even bigger mouths. Once a rumor gets started it seems to snowball until someone gets hurt. Everyone around here would be calling me loony and crazy if I mentioned my assessment of this case."

"So what did you come up with?" I asked, hoping he would confide in me.

And after a long minute of silence, he told me about his case: "I theorized that my subject ran away with another woman. … I found out that he was fooling around on his wife because they were constantly fighting and arguing with one another. And I figured he just got tired of all the bickering and yelling and left town with his new love. But his wife thought otherwise."

"So… what did she have to say about her husband's disappearance?"

"We didn't care about her input. We ended up closing the case."

"What do you <u>really</u> think happened to the woman's husband?" I asked.

"It doesn't matter what I think. I'll tell you this, though. The wife never believed her husband left with another woman. She'll tell you a different story. Instead of hearing it from me, I want you to drive out to this address and talk to the woman whose husband we investigated. Her name is Mrs. Dante. She will tell you a thing or two, if you can believe it," said Waters, eagerly handing me a piece of paper with Dante's name and address written on it.

"Well, let's hope she can fill in the blanks." I then placed the piece of paper in my jacket pocket for safekeeping.

"I'm sure she will tell you what's on her mind. She tells anyone who will listen."

With that said, I thanked Waters for his time and stood up to leave, saying, "Well, I have to get back to my department. I'll see you again, if I learn anything worth reporting."

I started to walk away but stopped as Detective Waters called out to me.

"Detective Zoolu. Have you heard about the 'Legend of Hollow Pass'?"

I turned to look at him, shrugged my shoulders and replied, "No, not really. I don't keep up with that fantasy crap. So I don't pay too much attention to that kind of stuff."

"Well, keep me informed of your investigation. I hope you find your partner. And Zoolu…if you need any help, don't hesitate to ask."

"Will do." I turned and quickly walked back to my department.

After sitting at my desk, dwelling over my situation, I decided to drive out to this woman's residence to see if I could learn anything of value about this strange costume shop. I still had a very bad feeling in the pit of my stomach. And it didn't go away as I drove out to the address Waters had given me. I just hoped it wasn't in a crazy area like the costume shop. I didn't think I could handle it today.

Her house was located in a large forest of giant trees within a large sub-division of mansions. An eerie mist surrounded it. The house was an exact replica of an old, English castle, but in miniature. It even had its own moat.

As I stepped out of the car and began walking across the bridge to the house, I noticed a little, white-haired old lady spying out of the picture window as she hid behind the curtains. I walked up to the front door and rang the doorbell. Seconds later, she answered it.

"Hello, Mrs. Dante…I'm Detective Zoolu," I said, showing her my police identification and gold shield.

Mrs. Dante invited me into her home. Standing in the foyer, I began noticing strange items in different areas of the house that supposedly kept away evil spirits – like garlic bulb necklaces hanging over many of the windows, and several religious statues – in prayer – placed as though they were standing guard.

This little, old woman was as eerie looking as the hunchbacked old man in the costume shop. She also had a hunchback, and a noticeable limp, long, white, stringy hair which partially covered her wrinkled, dimpled face and was only about four-and-a-half feet tall…but weighed a good one-hundred-and-fifty pounds and looked a hundred years old. I couldn't help but stare.

In fact, for a short time I was at a loss for words. But then remembered why I was there and spoke up.

"Mrs. Dante, I was talking to Detective Waters from Missing Person's concerning your husband's disappearance two years ago and he mentioned that I should speak with you concerning *my* partner's disappearance because I think your case and mine are connected. And I believe the old man from that costume shop is somehow involved in both of them."

She gave me a look that sent shivers through my spine, and in a deliberate, high voice, said, "What I know you may not want to here."

"No, on the contrary, I would like to hear what you have to say. Please, tell me."

I followed her through the house to her den, where we sat down and then she proceeded to tell me her story: "My family comes from the old country. They go back over six hundred years. You might as well know now that I'm a Gypsy...and a proud one at that. I'm telling you this now so you'll understand the whole story. And what I tell you is the truth, whether you believe me or not."

I gave her a look of confidence. "I have no reason not to believe you."

She smiled and then continued on with her story. "Before all this confusion exploded into my life...I was a beautiful, middle-aged woman. ... My nightmare began when my husband and I were riding around in our new car that we had just purchased a week before...and somehow got lost in a mountainous region and ended up in a desert."

"Didn't you plan your trip?"

"No, we were just going for a short ride. We were driving down the main highway when, all of a sudden, we found ourselves driving up a steep mountain road. I don't know how we got there. This area came out of nowhere. And the wind and fog was so bad we nearly wrecked our new car, that is until the devil grabbed hold of it and directed us to a ghost town. When my husband saw the costume shop sign...he thought it was fate that brought us there."

"Why do you say it was fate?"

"Because we had just been talking about renting costumes earlier, while riding in the car. We were going to our club's Halloween party…and only had a few days left to rent a costume. So this was the perfect place to rent them. But if I knew then, what I know now, I would never have set foot in that crazy costume shop. Or had any dealings with that hunchbacked man. I knew he was bad news as soon as we entered that place and saw him behind the counter, dressed up as a cowboy. And on the wall behind him was a small sign that cautioned all customers as to the rules of the store."

"What did the sign say?" I asked, as I couldn't remember seeing one.

"It stated that the costumes were one-of-a-kind and made from the most exquisite and rarest of materials. And that no deposit was required, but the costumes had to be worn out of the shop. And there were absolutely no returns or exchanges. I didn't really understand the rule about wearing the costumes out of the shop, so I asked the owner about it."

"Did he give you a hard time?"

"Not really. He answered my question cheerfully. He told us he wanted his customers to feel comfortable in their costumes so they wouldn't want to return them or exchange them for another…because he would have to either mend them or wash them if they were returned. He said the customers could try on as many different costumes as they wanted, as long as they did it in the store."

I asked her if she had tried on many costumes.

"I tried on a few different ones," was her answer.

"What did you think of them? Were they as well made as they looked?"

She replied, "Well, that man boasted that the costumes were one-of-a-kind. And most were very old and antique."

"What was your opinion of the owner?"

She told me that he was very eloquent in his speech, but very mysterious.

"How so?"

She thought for a second, and shrugged her shoulders. "I'm not sure. But he seemed to know what I was going to say before I said it. And he knew what costume my husband was going to pick out before my *husband* knew."

"Why do you say that?" I asked.

"Because he told my husband that he'd look perfect in a gangster's outfit. And then he pointed to a small cubicle in the far corner of the small room where we could change into our costumes."

"What did your husband do?"

She smiled and answered, "He just chuckled at the thought of dressing up as a gangster. But after looking at the rows and rows of some beautiful and exquisite costumes, he was drawn to one in particular."

"Which was?"

She snickered and replied, "A gangster costume! It was a nineteen-twenties-type black suit with spats that also included a shoulder holster with a thirty-eight-caliber revolver and a Thompson submachine gun. But that wasn't like my husband."

"Why? What should he have picked out?"

"He always liked to dress up as some type of soldier. Last year he picked a costume from the revolutionary war. But for some reason the gangster outfit mesmerized him. That hunchbacked old man told my husband that the costume had once belonged to John Dillinger."

"Did it?"

"I don't know, but my husband chuckled at that remark as he walked back to the small cubicle to change into his costume."

"You hadn't changed into *your* costume yet?"

"No. My husband changed first because I hadn't decided on what costume I wanted to wear. But while I was picking one out, another customer came into the shop along with her two young children. And the old man scolded her for letting her children run rampant through the shop."

"Did the old man seem that angry?"

"He was getting quite upset with her and her children. She tried to stop her kids from acting up, but for some reason...just couldn't control them. That's when I noticed the eyes of the old man began getting larger and larger when, all of a sudden they seemed to glow."

"Are you serious or are you just exaggerating?"

"No, sir. I actually thought they were gonna pop out of his skull. He directed his stare at the two uncontrollable children. And within a few seconds, the children had stopped acting silly and stood calmly right next to their mother, one on either side of her like little statues. The kids stood as if they were both in a deep trance. And then that little, strange shop became as quiet as a cemetery. That's when I knew that the old man had supernatural powers."

"What happened after that? Had your husband changed into his costume by then?"

"No...but by that time I had picked out *my* costume."

"What costume did you pick out?"

"I chose the Calamity Jane outfit.   And as soon as my husband came out of that changing room I told him what I had witnessed."

"What do you mean? Are you talking about the way the kids calmed down?"

"Yes, but my husband didn't seem to care. He was more interested about how he looked in his costume. I must say, he did look quite handsome in his gangster outfit – with the spats covering his shoes and his white, Panama straw hat covering his head. He looked very dapper. And under his jacket he carried a holstered gun, along with the submachine gun he carried in his hand. But for some reason his personality had completely changed."

"What do you mean, Mrs. Dante? How did he change?"

"He wasn't the nice, sweet, bashful person that I had known for thirty years, but a snotty, macho bully who filled his language with cuss words and obscenities. He was disgusting, but I thought he was just playing the part. You know, play acting."

"Was he?"

"I'm not certain to this day. I couldn't tell you."

"So what happened next," I asked her, "after he came out of the changing room?"

"He mentioned something about going outside to put his clothes into the car. But I needed his help with my dress so I ran out of the changing room to get him before he left, but he was practically out the front door by the time I saw him."

"You changed into your costume that fast?"

"No. I came out because I couldn't reach the buttons on the back of my dress. I was walking behind him, trying to get his attention so he could help me with it, but I guess he didn't hear me and walked out the shop's front door, shutting it behind him. But just before it closed I noticed a real bright flash of white light that nearly blinded me."

Suddenly, Mrs. Dante stopped in the middle of the conversation to catch her breath.

"Did you pass out or did you go after him?" I asked.

She stayed quiet for a few seconds, then answered: "Just as the door was about to close I grabbed hold of it. I had it open about a half an inch, when I thought I saw a gang of thugs, all carrying machine guns. I thought I even heard gunshots and the rapid firing of machine guns."

"Excuse me … What did you say? You saw some other gangsters shooting at your husband? Is that what you're saying, Mrs. Dante?"

"Yes. That's **exactly** what I'm saying!"

"You're sure you didn't dream this? Or maybe that bright light that you say you witnessed had something to do with your delusion?"

"Don't treat me like a child, Detective. I know what I saw," snapped Mrs. Dante.

"So... what did you do when you saw what was happening to your husband?"

"I tried to open the door to get a better view but the two small children standing nearby began fighting and fell against it, closing it. I quickly opened it, but by then...there wasn't anything to see."

"Was your car still there?"

She shook her head. "No car, no husband, no gangsters with machine guns, nothing. That's when I must have fainted, because the next thing I remembered...was someone tugging at my clothes and slapping my face."

"Who was it that was standing over you?"

"I think it was the hunchbacked, old man. I screamed at him to give me back my husband."

"Why would he take your husband? That's silly."

"I don't know why! But I'm telling you. That evil man took my husband away from me."

"Mrs. Dante, how can you say that?"

"Listen. After I saw him zap those two little kids with his weird, telepathic powers, I knew he was evil...and the one responsible for my husband's disappearance."

"Did you ask him about it?"

"Yes, but when I began to rant and rave, that's when he must have zapped me, too. From that moment on, I couldn't remember anything. I couldn't even remember how I got home that night."

"Did you talk with anyone about your weird experience?"

"Yes. I know I talked with the authorities, but I can't remember a thing. I must have been home a good one or two days before my senses returned."

"You honestly believe that the man from the costume shop has some magical, evil powers?" I asked her, adding, "That's a lot of superstition!"

"You say it's a lot of hogwash, hey, Detective Zoolu?" asked Mrs. Dante, as she walked over to the other side of her living room.

"I do."

"Let me show you something." She then picked up a framed picture off one of her end tables and handed it to me, which showed a beautiful, blond woman in her late-twenties or early-thirties.

I asked her if the woman in the picture was her daughter.

She replied, "No, Detective Zoolu. That is a picture of me almost five years ago. Would you believe I am thirty-six years old? But look at me now. I look like an old woman of eighty. And I feel like an old woman of eighty. But before I entered that costume shop, I looked exactly like the woman in the framed picture."

"Don't take this wrong, Mrs. Dante, but maybe you have some rare disease."

She snickered, shook her head to and fro, then said, "Thirty days after I left that costume shop, my aging began. Two years later, I looked like this." Pointing to herself.

"Mrs. Dante, what did your doctor say?"

"What could he say? He doesn't understand what's happening to my body either."

We were getting off the subject so I asked her about her husband. "What did the police investigators say about your husband's disappearance?"

"They said he ran away with another woman."

"Mrs. Dante, did you tell them your story?"

She gave me a dirty look. "Of course I did. But your police department thought I was crazy and just imagining things. They blamed my husband's disappearance on our failed marriage."

"That does sound much more plausible than *your* theory."

"Oh yeah! Well I say...the police would rather close a case than investigate it properly and thoroughly. They didn't believe me and came to the conclusion that my husband ran away with some other woman."

"Don't take this the wrong way, Mrs. Dante, but maybe he did and you're just in denial."

"Let me tell you about me and my husband, Detective Zoolu," she replied rather sternly. "We grew up together, since kindergarten. And I might add, for more than thirty years, were quite fond of each other. But don't get me wrong. We did have our ups and downs…just like any normal couple. Even so, Detective, we were still in love with each other."

"You might have been in love with him, but was *he* in love with you?"

She gave me a cold look. "We had quarrels and a few love spats during our marriage, but what couple doesn't go through that every now and then? My husband and I sometimes fought like cats and dogs, but it was never physical. Usually, we kept it to yelling and screaming."

"Did your husband have any girlfriends or mistresses that you know of?"

"My husband had a few affairs over the years, but we managed to work it out. He would always come back to me and I would always take him back…because I believe in the sanctity of marriage. Like I said, we were in love with each other, even though your police department thinks otherwise."

"But maybe he *did* go away with one of his girlfriends?"

"Detective, you don't just throw thirty years of love and friendship out the window. I promised myself that one day I was gonna go back to that costume shop and confront that old man. I want to wear one of those costumes and see what happens to me."

"Why do that? What would that accomplish? It would just bring back bad memories."

She insisted. "If I could talk my sister into driving me out there I would go back this instant."

"I think you're being foolish, Mrs. Dante. You should just let the police investigators handle it. You're just gonna make yourself depressed. It's not worth the aggravation."

"I know what I've been saying sounds far-fetched, Detective Zoolu, but it's the gospel truth. My husband would never have left me for another woman. We trusted each other implicitly."

I listened intently to her crazy story for over an hour, but took it with a grain of salt. I thought the old woman was a raving lunatic…and in need of some electric shock therapy. I was sure she wasn't playing with a full deck. She thought that little, fat, hunchbacked, old man was some kind of sorcerer that had conjured up a spell to make her husband disappear. But I didn't believe in all that hocus-pocus.

I figured if this old man was involved in these disappearances, then he either killed these people or had someone else do it for him. Then, he probably took all their money and valuables so he could sell them, along with their vehicles. I was positive that there was nothing mysterious about it. And I had heard everything I needed to hear. Mrs. Dante had been quite entertaining, if nothing else.

But I had work to do and wanted to get back to the station…because it was near quitting time. And tomorrow, I would return to the scene of the crime – to talk to that little, scruffy boy…and to the old man again. Basically, I just wanted to nose around.

So I thanked Mrs. Dante for her time, adding, "If I hear anything more about your husband, I will surely let you know. If I can be of further service, please don't hesitate to contact me at the station." I then handed her my business card.

Soon after, she escorted me to the front door, saying, "I know you don't believe a word I've told you, Detective, but believe me…it's the truth."

"I believe you, Mrs. Dante."

"Well, I hope I've been some help to your investigation."

I smiled and nodded, then said, "Goodbye, Mrs. Dante…and take care." I then walked out the front door to my car.

I couldn't wait to get home to relax and have a few strong drinks. This case was taking its toll on me. I couldn't get it out of my mind…because it was always interrupting my thoughts.

So five minutes after reaching the station, I signed out and raced home to fill my head with liquid dreams.

CHAPTER 3

Once at home, I went directly to my kitchen cabinet and pulled out my twenty-year old bottle of scotch. And as soon as I went into the living room and sat down on the couch, I began exercising my right arm by throwing back shot after shot of it down my gullet. Within an hour or so, I wasn't feeling anything. My body felt totally numb.

I tried not to think about my case but I couldn't help myself. My thoughts constantly returned to my partner's disappearance. He had disappeared just like Dante's husband had. And I was pretty convinced that the two bodies were laying six feet under…in the desert and within earshot of that strange, dilapidated, ghost town. But I was confused. Did that desert really exist?

Suddenly, I became very dizzy…and the room began spinning round and round. It just wouldn't stop. Seconds later, I began getting an upset stomach. So I got up to go to the bathroom and that was the last thing I remembered until the next morning when I woke up with my head lying on the toilet seat. Boy, did I have a stiff neck and sore back.

I showered, shaved, dressed and then made a pot of strong, black coffee, pouring cup after cup into my body…trying to resurrect myself from the dead. That's how bad I felt: Like the living dead. But it was time to go to work. So I slowly stumbled out my front door, down the steps and to my car, driving directly to the station.

Ten minutes after leaving my abode, I arrived at my destination. And after signing in at the front desk I walked to the snack room and poured myself a big cup of awful-tasting, black coffee. Once I felt strong enough, I left the station and headed towards that strange, little, ghost town once again, driving in the same direction as I had the day before.

Nearly two hours later, the main road suddenly disappeared and I found myself driving up the same narrow mountain road I had the day before.

And again I seemed to have run into Mother Nature's wrath. The wind seemed to puff up and blow with hurricane proportions, shaking my car from one side of the road to the other and pushing it near the edge of the ravine, while storm clouds and foggy mist covered the entire area making it impossible to see.

The weather was foggy and cloudy, and so too was my mind. I was trying to figure out what was happening to me when, all of a sudden, I found myself unable to move and no longer in control of my body, just like the day before. Something had control of me…of my mind, my body … And my car. Every time I tried to fight my phantom attacker, it consumed more of me. I couldn't get control of myself or my car…until I had landed at the bottom of the canyon. Then I drove the three miles into town…very slowly.

I was hoping to see someone … Anyone. But the town seemed bare. Not a soul around. But then, I noticed the same small, dirty boy that I had seen before, jump out from behind one of the deserted buildings and head into the costume shop carrying in his arms, a rather large bundle. I quickly parked the car and followed the boy into the shop, just a few seconds behind him.

Entering the building, I looked to see where the boy was…because I wanted to talk with him. But I didn't see him. Where was he hiding, I thought to myself? There was no back room to escape to. Was he hiding in the changing room? I walked over to the far corner of the small, crowded room and quickly looked into the small cubicle. But to my surprise, he wasn't there either. I quickly glanced around the rest of the room, checking behind each one of the mannequins, but the boy was nowhere to be found.

I was getting very frustrated and thought I was losing my mind. I just couldn't think straight. What the heck was going on? Now I was adamant at finding that little boy. I had some very important questions to ask him.

Jackson Billing, the old hunchback, sat behind his little counter and acted as though I was crazy. But he didn't say a word. He just kept staring at me with his big, bulging eyes, straining to pop out of their eye sockets. I ignored his stare and nonchalantly checked behind some of the costume racks to see if the boy was hiding there. But he wasn't. In fact, I didn't see him anywhere. I must be losing my mind, I thought to myself.

Then I stared at the old man…trying to read his thoughts. That's when I noticed the costume in front of him lying across the counter. And it seemed to be the same color material that I had seen the boy carrying. Now I was sure that the boy had entered the shop…and I knew that I wasn't seeing things and my mind hadn't been playing tricks on me.

The old man must have read my mind…because he quickly placed the costume in a small drawer behind the counter. Evidently, he didn't want me to examine it. So, for the time being, I played along with his little charade.

"Mr. Billing, where is the boy?" I asked.

"What boy?" he replied, his bulging eyes peering through his thick-lensed, wire-framed glasses.

"The boy I followed into your shop. He came in a few minutes before me…carrying a small bundle of material. The same color as the costume you just hid from me. Where is he?"

"I don't know who you mean? I didn't see any little boy come into my shop. I don't allow any children in here unless accompanied by an adult. Look around. Do you see any little boy? I don't. All I see is you and me, Mister. Are you sure you're feeling alright?"

I was becoming very angry and irritated by his stupid denials.

"Don't give me any of that crap, Mr. Billing. Do you have a back door in this joint?" I asked, pacing around the room, trying to find a hidden door or a phony wall.

He had to be here, I thought. Somewhere? But where?

"Mister," snorted Billings, "I am telling you the truth. No boy came into my shop today. We are the only ones here."

Just as he said that, a lovely, beautiful, young woman walked into the shop. She glanced around the room and closed the door behind her. She looked at us two old men, who were stunned by her beauty, and smiled. She melted our hearts, at least mine…that's for sure.

"Don't let me interrupt you," said the smiling, beautiful, young female customer. "Please continue with whatever you were doing. I just want to look at all these beautiful costumes."

As the young woman walked past us, Mr. Billing and I stared at her exquisite shape. She was definitely a knockout. But my attention quickly returned to the hunchbacked, old man once again.

"Mr. Billing, is there a back door to this place?" I asked, not seeing one.

"Yes, but it hasn't been opened in years," he replied, pointing in the direction of the back door.

I walked to the back of the small shack to check the door. I had to move some of the racks of costumes out of the way before I could even get to it. The costumes didn't look like they had been touched and the door was definitely locked…with a heavy chain and pad lock. This door hadn't been used in years, just like the old man had said…because there were cobwebs in every corner of the doorjamb. The boy couldn't possibly have gone this way.

As I beat my head against the wall, wondering where the kid went to, I noticed the young woman looking over my shoulder. She was browsing through the many racks of costumes, selecting different items from each one. I still wondered who this young woman was. I thought she might have been the old man's daughter – that is, until she asked him about renting his costumes. She seemed very inquisitive and interested in his costume shop…and after reading the sign on the wall – the one behind the counter that Mrs. Dante had mentioned and I had failed to see, she began asking Billing many questions concerning his costumes.

"Why do you use such exquisite and exotic material in your costumes?" the young woman asked Billing. "Are they really one of a kind?"

"Yes," he replied. "We only make one of each and we make them to look as realistic and authentic as the originals."

"Your sign says that there is no security deposit needed to rent your costumes. Is that true?" asked the beautiful, young woman.

"Yes, that's true. The only condition in store policy is that you must wear the costume out of the shop. We don't allow returns or exchanges."

"Why is that?" she asked in her sweet, sultry low voice.

While Billing and the young woman talked, I continued looking and checking behind the racks of costumes…hoping to find the boy hiding. But he was nowhere in sight. So I gave up the hunt and stood behind a row of costumes near the counter, listening intently to the conversation between the old man and young woman.

"We find," said Billing, "that once the customer wears the costume and feels comfortable in it, he won't want to wear any other costume. You really didn't want to rent a costume today anyway, did you?"

Billing seemed to be eyeing the young woman suspiciously, as though he was reading her mind, while she came across as though she was flirting with the old geezer.

"How did you know? You must be a mind reader. I just wanted to ask you some questions about your shop. I was thinking of opening one similar to yours in *my* little town."

Yeah… I thought to myself. She wants to know about his shop and so do I. But not in the same way. I was interested in Billing…she was interested in him and he seemed to be interested in her.

"Where did you buy your exotic material that you use to make your costumes?" she asked the old man. "Do you make the costumes or do you have them made for you?"

As I waited to hear the answer, I noticed the front door open. To my surprise, the little boy I had been hunting for…walked up to the counter and asked the old man a question. I couldn't hear what was said, but the old man quickly grabbed a few bills out of the cash register and handed them to him. The boy grabbed the bills, stuck them into his jacket pocket and quickly turned towards the front door.

I tried to stop him from leaving, but as I reached out to grab him, I stumbled and knocked over one of the mannequins. And by the time I had picked it up and replaced the hat on its head, the boy was gone. But only a few seconds had passed. That's why, when I opened the door, I was taken aback…because I was staring into an empty street. I didn't see the boy anywhere. So I stepped outside and ran from one side of the building to the other, but still no boy. I shook my head in disbelief and utter amazement. A few minutes later…I peered into the shop, standing just outside the front door, hoping the boy had returned. But he hadn't.

Again I ran from one side of the building to the other…but saw nothing. Then I ran completely around the dilapidated shop…but saw only cactus and tumbleweeds. I became a little frightened by what was happening to me… and was beginning to doubt my own sanity.

That kid couldn't have moved that fast, I thought to myself. He would have to be as fast as lightning. Giving up my hunt…I stood outside the shop shaking my head in disbelief and utter disgust…because I couldn't believe that that kid had gotten away from me.

After a few minutes of fuming, I re-entered the costume shop. And as I did, I noticed the old man…cleaning and repairing another costume. Then, looking around the little shop, I noticed the young woman was gone. But I figured she was in the changing room trying on a costume.

I then walked over to the counter and began questioning the hunchbacked and bug-eyed, old man, Jackson Billing.

"Mr. Billing, where does that boy live?"

"I don't know? What boy are you talking about?" he replied, peering over his thick-lensed, wire-rimmed glasses.

"I don't know what you're trying to hide, Mr. Billing. But I'm not amused."

"I'm not hiding anything, detective."

"You don't fool me, sir. I will find out eventually."

Just as I was about to ask another question, my throat began burning as if on fire, just as it had the day before. The burning sensation went all the way from my throat down to the pit of my stomach. I felt nauseated, fatigued and dizzy. Every time I tried to speak…it was like breathing in a forest fire. I didn't understand what was happening to me and stared into the little, old man's eyes hoping he would give me an answer. But it seemed as though he was in a deep trance. And then I saw his body become hideously distorted and his face turn a beet red. Suddenly my dizziness progressed, so much so, I thought I was going to faint. My tie seemed to choke me to the point I couldn't breathe. I had to get out of that strange shop…as quickly as possible. Something was very odd. In fact, I believed something or someone was trying to kill me.

I then turned and ran out of the shop. But it seemed as though it took me five minutes to take the twenty steps to the front door. And when I was finally outside in the fresh air…I was able to take a deep breath, even though my esophagus still burned as I inhaled the cool air into my parched lungs. At that moment, I decided I had to leave that strange, little town.

So I jumped into my car even though I was still feeling dizzy and very fatigued. Then, after starting its engine, stepped down on the accelerator to flee…but the car wouldn't respond. Again, I pressed the gas pedal to the floor…but it still wouldn't move. The car had a mind of its own. Finally, after what seemed like hours, the car suddenly lurched forward…and I was finally heading out of that spooky, crazy town, never wanting to return. But I knew I had to…because I had a job to do. And that was to find my missing partner.

My throat and stomach continued to burn and it was hard for me to breathe and swallow. Now I wondered if I was going to end up looking like Mrs. Dante…a thirty-six year old woman that looked eighty. I was more frightened at what I didn't know than by what I did.

About a mile away from that strange town, I noticed what seemed to be a very large, brown, grizzly bear walking on the side of the road. This wasn't the type of terrain for grizzly bears...or any bears, for that matter. They couldn't survive out here, unless they could eat cactus and tumbleweeds.

But the closer I got, the mysterious bear became clearer to me. It wasn't a bear at all, but a very large man wearing a bearskin coat walking in the direction I was traveling. I stepped on the brakes to stop. I wanted to ask him if he needed a ride, but the car refused to respond. As the car slowly passed him, the big man didn't even notice my car. I could see he was an old, Indian man. I didn't have any idea where he was walking to because there wasn't a teepee or building in the nearby area. Looking into my rear-view mirror as I passed him, the old Indian became smaller and smaller until he just disappeared.

Suddenly, the car jerked and began to respond to my actions. That is, until I reached the mountain. Then, once again, someone or something had complete control of my car and my body.

This was beginning to drive me dizzy. I was glad it was the end of the workweek, because I would have the weekend to relax my brain. But right now, I was struggling to get back control of my senses and control of my car. And as the car climbed up the mountain road, the weather once again became very demonic.

Mother Nature seemed pissed...because her howling, racing winds began tossing my car from one lane to the other, at times pushing it to the edge of the cliff...and then before falling into the ravine below, the car would suddenly swerve back to the other side of the road and towards the side of the rocky mountain...but for some reason...just stop short of crashing into it. If there had been any other cars coming towards me during this time, it would have been disastrous.

But that wasn't the half of it. Suddenly, something different and unexpected happened. The cloudy and foggy skies began spitting hail balls of ice as big as jumbo eggs. My car was being pounded and pelted by these bullets from Mother Nature's gun. This had never happened before. At least, I couldn't remember it happening before. Although my car's body had been in excellent condition, now it looked as though someone had hit it with a hundred big rocks…and had been in a war.

As the car continued its climb up the steep and winding mountain road, the fog became so thick that it became impossible to see – just like before. And I still had no control over my car. Finally, I had reached the peak of the mountain and was now going down this winding road, heading towards the main highway, which was still hidden behind the fog and clouds. But as the car roared down the steep road, the crazy weather ***finally*** began to subside.

The farther away I got from that area the more normal things became. As the cloudy mist and fog evaporated, the main highway suddenly appeared. Just at that moment…I was once again in control of my car … And my faculties.

I quickly looked into my rear-view mirror and noticed the mountain had also disappeared, as though it had never existed. I stomped on the accelerator, damn near putting my foot through the floorboard. I wanted to get away from that area as quickly as possible. And then I had the whole weekend to sober up and regain my sanity. Right at this moment…I didn't know whether I was coming or going?

I honestly thought I was losing my mind. I should have asked one of those costume shop customers if they had gone through the same gates of hell to get to that costume shop as I had. But not knowing how they would react to my questions I thought against it. I didn't want to be known as the lunatic detective. I had heard enough of that from my peers in my department. I think Detective Waters had the same fear?

None of this made any sense to me. I didn't believe in sorcerers, ghouls, ghosts or goblins. I went with the norm…and made decisions on hard evidence. If I had told anyone about what I had seen or even what I thought I had seen, the boys in white coats would have taken me away to the nut house and thrown away the key. My job as a detective would have come to an abrupt ending if that had happened. So, for now, I was going to keep my mouth shut.

When I finally reached the station it was so late that all I did was sign in at the front desk and sign back out. Then I went straight home to relax … And drink.

As I was leaving the station one of the other detectives saw me and expressed his opinion.

"Man, Zoolu, you better go home and rest up. You look like crap. It looks like you've been run over by a big, Mac truck. What's gotten into you today?" he asked as I tried to ignore him.

"Huh? What? Yeah, I must be coming down with the flu or some kind of virus. I have two days to bombard it with antibiotics," I lied.

I quickly walked away from the detective and headed out the front door to my car. I couldn't drive home fast enough…and made it there in record time. And the first thing that I did when I got inside…was to go directly to the kitchen cabinet and pull out my twenty-year-old bottle of scotch – again. But this time…it was nearly empty, so I pulled out another bottle from a case that I kept locked up in my closet. And then…I walked back into the kitchen and poured myself a stiff drink. A few seconds after I downed the triple shot of scotch, sweat began to pour out of my body.

So I walked to the bathroom, turned on the faucet and splashed some water on my face…then glanced into the bathroom mirror…and noticed something different about myself. My face seemed to have a few more wrinkles than it had before leaving the house this morning.

I then flashed back to the interview I had with Mrs. Dante, who had aged fifty years over a two year period…which happened after she had visited that crazy costume shop. I started to think that this aging disease or whatever it was…was now beginning to take hold of my body, too. I splashed more water onto my face hoping I would awaken from my dream, but then quickly realized…that I _was_ awake.

I was becoming too paranoid, I thought. All this talk about strange happenings and sorcerers was starting to get under my skin.

"But I don't believe in all that garbage," I said out loud. "I don't believe in all that hocus pocus. Do you hear me?" I yelled these words at the top of my voice...for anyone to hear...especially the trolls and spirits.

Then I had to chuckle at myself for acting so immature and stupid.

I returned to the living room and began exercising my right arm...by pouring stiff drinks and downing them one after another. I counted ten before passing out on the couch. This time though, I didn't awaken in the middle of the night from my nightmares as I had done previously. But I still had the weekend to conquer.

I slept damn near till noon...and had never slept that long in my life. Not even in my youth. But instead of feeling wide-awake, I felt rather sluggish and tired. How could that be, I thought? Then I remembered – the alcohol!

I tried to put the investigation out of my mind. But it just didn't seem to work. The only way I could forget my troubles was to drown them in liquor. So I drank scotch from Friday night through Sunday night. And stayed numb all weekend long. That seemed to do the trick in helping me forget about my investigation. In fact, I couldn't remember having one nightmare on the subject. Actually...I couldn't remember anything during those few days.

However, when I awoke on Monday morning, I looked in the mirror to shave and got quite a shock. My face had aged overnight. And my hair had started changing colors – from a dirt gray to a snow white. I tried pulling out each white hair that I saw, but there were just too many...and due to my enormous hangover, my eyes weren't quite focused yet...to do the job adequately.

Ignoring my new added features…I quickly showered, shaved and dressed – and in the same clothes that I had slept in – then drove directly to the station…forgetting about breakfast and coffee in the process.

CHAPTER 4

Once inside the station, I quickly signed in at the front desk and then walked straight to my desk while many of my peers stared at my disheveled body. I still had a heavy hangover. So much so, that the room was spinning.

I needed a cup of strong, hot, black coffee right away to get me out of my doldrums. So before sitting down in my chair I turned and walked to the snack room and then poured two cups of coffee down my gullet within five minutes. I needed to wake up and wake up fast because I wanted to look for my partner's case files again – at least that would keep me away from that crazy costume shop today.

I wasn't in any mood to go out there – especially knowing that I'd have to defend myself against Mother Nature's stormy episodes at Devil's Mountain – because my head was still fogged in from my weekend of binge drinking. That's what I started calling that area: Devil's Mountain. I thought the name was appropriate.

Today I just wanted to stay around the station and get my head on straight...even though my peers and co-workers kept staring at me and giving me weird looks. I really didn't care...because they were always hassling me about my binge drinking and hangovers.

And I did have a horrendous hangover this particular morning. However, within a few hours it had subsided. That's when I began looking for my missing partner's case files in earnest. I looked behind water coolers, desks and any other place I thought he might have laid his notebook of case files. But came away empty-handed.

I had just about given up on finding any information that might have helped me with my investigation when I decided to take a restroom break. So I walked to the bathroom and washed my hands and face. Then went and sat in my favorite stall. And just as I bent down to place a sanitary paper covering over the toilet seat, I saw a dusty notebook hidden behind the toilet bowl. I quickly pulled it out from its hiding spot and glanced through it. Sure enough, it was my partner's notebook containing his present case files. He had been working on two different homicides. Plus, he had a file that he had started on his own without the knowledge of his superiors – the disappearance of one of his closest neighbors: an ex-girlfriend.

Just as I began reading the notebook, my captain walked into the restroom. So I decided it was time to get back to work…and stuffed the notebook into my jacket pocket before walking past him.

"How are you doing, Captain?" I asked, standing near the wash basin.

"I'm doing fine. But how are *you* doing, Zoolu?" he retorted, having heard about my nauseated hangover.

"I'm doing better now, sir."

"How is your case coming on the disappearance of Detective Webber? Have you come up with any answers yet?"

"No sir, not yet," I lied.

I didn't want to tell Captain Bird what I really thought was happening…because I didn't want him to pull me off the case and throw me into a mental institution. He would have thought that I was loony tunes, especially if I explained to him about Devil's Mountain and that crazy, hunchback, Jackson Billing.

"Well, let me know as soon as you have something concrete," said Bird.

"Will do, Captain. Now I have to get back to my investigation."

With that said I left the restroom. And then, while walking back to my desk, I noticed a man talking to Sergeant Labor at the front desk. I was curious and stood to one side of the counter so I could overhear the conversation they were having. The man speaking was a detective from a city near the state line, eighty miles to the east, who worked out of Missing Person's and was investigating a few different disappearances. His investigation had brought him to this area searching for clues. He was looking for a costume shop that his victim's spouse had described to him…but couldn't locate it. When I heard that I decided it was time to introduce myself.

"Hi, I'm homicide detective Brad Zoolu…and I'm also investigating a disappearance, my partner's."

"I'm glad to meet you, Mr. Zoolu…I'm Detective Matthew," he replied, in a deep, booming voice, while shaking my outstretched hand. "I work out of Paris Police station, just a few miles away from the state line."

"Let's take a walk and talk. Excuse me if I seem sluggish. I had a rough weekend. I'm taking it easy today," I said, not wanting to reveal my weakness for booze.

"That sounds all right to me. But I can't stay too long. I have to question one or two more witnesses today. But as I was telling Sergeant Labor…I'm looking for a costume shop that is supposed to be in a very small town out in the desert. The only problem is, there isn't any desert…at least not on any map that I looked at."

"Detective Matthew, why did you come to <u>this</u> police station?" I asked, yawning and rubbing my eyes as we walked outside to the courtyard.

"I was told by one of my eyewitnesses that this costume shop was supposedly a few hours from this city. But when I looked on the road map there was nothing like my witness had described. So, I decided to stop here and ask."

"I hope I don't disappoint you."

"Can you help me?" he asked.

"I think I can."

"Maybe you can draw me a map, if it's not too much trouble for you?"

"Sure, I can do that for you. Better yet, I'll even drive you out there."

"I don't want to inconvenience you. I can drive out there myself."

"Detective Matthew, I don't think you would want to drive out there by yourself. Especially if you run into the same bad weather that I have crossed paths with. If you go out there alone…no one will ever believe your story about that town and that costume shop. You'll need me as a witness."

"I haven't told anyone this," Matthew whispered. "But my eyewitnesses have told me some unbelievable things about that place. But I just thought they were upset over their loss. I really didn't pay any attention to their crazy stories. That's why I need to see for myself."

As we stopped walking and sat down on a bench, I added, "Some of the peculiar things that have happened to me out there, I don't even want to discuss with you. I want you to witness it for yourself. I want you to question your own sanity, not mine."

I didn't want to reveal anything that might sound too far-fetched or crazy. And I didn't want to tell him anything about my case. He wasn't in my jurisdiction. But I was very interested in what he had to say.

And surprised when he told me that he'd like to go with me today, but didn't have the time.

I was relieved to hear him say that…and replied, "I can't go there today either. Well, not can't, but I don't want to go out there today. I don't think I could handle the confusion today. By the time I get back from that place I'm dazed and confused."

"Gee," he said gleefully, "I can't wait to visit that town. It sounds very interesting and mysterious. My eyewitnesses don't even know how they got there. They say that all of a sudden, as they were driving on the main thoroughfare, a mountainous, dirt road suddenly appeared out of nowhere. Is that true, Zoolu?"

"I don't want to tell you. I want you to experience it for yourself and then you can tell me what you've experienced and saw."

"Well, I'm going to be busy for the next few days, but I will come back near the end of the week. If I can get back sooner I'll telephone and let you know."

"Detective Matthew, do you still want me to draw you a map just in case you don't get back this way … Or do you want to just wait and ride along with me?"

He thought for a moment, then said, "I'll just wait and ride along with you. I can always have you fax me a copy of the map if I need it. If I have to experience a mysterious intervention I would rather be with someone…than alone, and that way…when I write my report I can have confirmation from a credible witness. In fact, if you have the time, maybe you can help me out and question one of my eyewitnesses for me."

"Yes, I could do that," I told him.

Matthew continued: "I would like you to hear this woman's story. I have already asked her a few questions surrounding her husband's disappearance. But I think she has a screw loose."

But I wondered why he didn't want to come along to interview her?

He replied, "Because I still need to question a person who is related to a couple who has also disappeared. All of these missing people had thought about or talked about renting costumes for upcoming parties, but not from any particular costume shop. But somehow all of them ended up at this one. Like I said before, the witnesses who I've already interviewed didn't even know how they got to that shop. And for some unexplained reasons, the missing victims never returned to their homes."

"Detective Matthew, when did you start your investigations?"

"I just started my investigation on two missing persons a few days ago when I questioned my first eyewitness, who was either mentally ill or just plain crazy. That's why I want you to question that witness," he said, looking at his watch. "Jeez, it's after lunchtime already. I have to get. I have to track down a few of these eyewitnesses before the day ends. And at this rate, I won't get back to my office until dinner time."

"Detective Matthew, do you want to be my guest for lunch? Then we can talk over our cases and delve into them a little deeper."

"Let me take a rain check on that. Next time I'm here, maybe we'll have lunch before we ride out to that costume shop? But I'm going to have to leave now."

As he stood up he handed me the name and address of the person he wanted me to question.

"Will do," I said, taking the paper out of his hand.

"And I want you to tell me what you think of my eyewitness's story when I come back later this week."

I nodded, then walked him to his car and told him that I'd try and question his witness within the next few days. "That is, if I don't get caught up in an emergency situation. But I don't see that happening, not if I can help it."

"Thanks for everything, Detective Zoolu."

"Well Detective Matthew, I'll see you at the end of the week," I said, shaking his hand.

"My friends call me John." He then entered his car and started its engine.

"My friends call me Detective Zoolu," I replied laughing, as we waved goodbye to each other.

I waited a few seconds, watching him leave the parking lot and then returned to my desk…to look over my missing partner's case files. But just as I began that quest, a middle-aged woman came into the station screaming and whining, and ranting and raving. Something about her sister suddenly disappearing, just like her husband had two years earlier…and that her sister had followed her husband's footsteps trying to find out where he had gone. But now, she had disappeared, too. I really couldn't understand her due to her mumbling, crying, and stuttering. But I had to find out what happened. So I walked over to her and introduced myself.

"Hello, I'm Detective Zoolu," I said, patting her shoulder, as I tried to calm her down. "Why don't we go into the interview room and talk about your situation." As I slowly directed the upset woman towards the interview room she continued to cry and mutter to herself. As we entered the room, I asked her to sit down and tell me her problems. "Now, tell me what is bothering you?"

"Are you Detective Zoolu?" asked the woman, finally settling down.

"Yes…I'm Detective Brad Zoolu."

"You can call me Debby. My sister talked about you the other day."

"Oh? And who is your sister?"

"You know her as Mrs. Dante."

"Oh, yes. We talked about her husband's disappearance."

"Yes I know. My sister was so obsessed with finding her husband she never stopped talking about his disappearance. I guess when you came over and questioned her…it brought back all her terrible nightmares. Her obsession with her husband's disappearance began to gnaw at her again."

"Why, what happened?" I asked, wanting to hear her story.

"Just after you left her house, she began calling me at all hours of the day and night and begged me to drive her to that costume shop. Even though she didn't know how to get there, she wanted to try anyway."

"Didn't you try and stop her?"

"Of course I tried to talk her out of it. But she was adamant. She was going to get there by hell or high water. She talked about nothing else but her missing husband. She wanted to be where he was. She felt her time was running out."

Mrs. Dante's sister sat in her chair dazed and confused…staring straight ahead, not looking at anything in particular as though she was in a trance.

"Miss, are you all right?" I asked her.

She suddenly snapped out of it, saying, "You saw how old my sister looked, didn't you? She wanted her questions answered before she died. She wanted to be with her husband…right next to his side. She believed that somehow…if she wore a costume similar to the one he wore, she would be in the same part of time as he was in. I felt sick every time she talked that way. I kept begging her to think clearly and realistically and to listen to what she was saying." Tears started welling up in her eyes.

"What did she say to that?"

"She believed some type of time warp was involved in her husband's disappearance. She believed when the front door of that costume shop was opened at that particular time, the time warp came into play. But she wasn't very sure. That's why she wanted to try her theory out on herself." She shook her head in disbelief and frustration, adding, "Her story didn't make any sense to me."

I nodded and said, "She didn't make much sense to me, either."

"But what about her aging? When you see a young, beautiful, thirty-six year old woman change into an eighty year old, practically overnight, what is one to think?"

"I'm not sure what to think," I answered.

"Then how do you account for her appearance?" she interjected. "Something weird happened to her at that costume shop."

"Did she tell you that, Debby or were you just reading between the lines?"

"She's my sister. I know her like the back of my hand. We were very close," she cried.

"Did your sister really believe that stuff she was spewing...or did she believe her husband ran off with another woman?" I asked, trying to test her reaction to my question.

She thought for a minute, then replied, "Well, now that you put it that way, I don't know? The way she rambled on, I really thought she believed her husband had disappeared. Not once did she say that someone had killed her husband. She actually thought the old man at the costume shop had something to do with the time warp that made her husband disappear. She thought he was a sorcerer or witch doctor."

"You don't believe that, do you, Debby?"

"Remember, she is a Gypsy. We believe in the supernatural."

"So how did your sister get out to that place if she doesn't have a car?"

"She begged _me_ to take her, but when I refused...she asked her next door neighbor to rent her a car."

"Why didn't she rent her own car?"

She shrugged her shoulders, and said, "I guess she made up some lame excuse about not having a valid credit card, so the neighbor rented one for her."

"Did the neighbor drive her out there?"

"No. I guess she drove herself there."

"But I thought she didn't drive?"

"She didn't <u>like</u> to drive. Because she didn't have a driver's license. She hadn't driven in over ten years."

"Why was that?" I asked her.

"Because she just didn't like to drive. I guess she was afraid."

"Well, don't take this wrong…but <u>I</u> thought your sister had a screw loose. I think losing her husband probably drove her to a nervous breakdown."

"Then what happened to her husband?" whined Debby.

"Her husband was an adulterer. So he's probably living with another woman as we speak. Because we know for a fact that he had many affairs with younger women…and probably started a new life and new family."

She shook her head no, saying, "I don't think so."

"Either that…or that old man at the costume shop killed him and buried him in the desert," I added.

"I don't believe that! And I don't believe my sister had a nervous breakdown either!"

"Your sister's problem…is she can't comprehend his leaving her for another woman. She just won't face the facts. If your sister did drive out there, I hope she didn't drive her car off a cliff into the deep ravine?"

"Is that what you think happened to my sister?"

I shrugged my shoulders and replied, "I don't know. But one thing I do know…she sure didn't go through any time warp. I'll have the County Sheriff and the State Police check the sides of the roads and highways leading in the direction of that costume shop."

"Do you think they will find her?"

"If she crashed on the way, we'll find her and the car she was driving. I just hope we can find her alive?"

"One thing is for sure though."

"What's that, Debby?"

"My sister is only thirty-six years old, but has the body of an eighty year old woman. That is reality. You can't deny that something or someone destroyed her beautiful face and body…and it practically happened over night."

"Maybe she caught some rare disease?"

"You just don't get it, do you, Detective? Before she visited that mysterious costume shop, she had the body of a sparkling, young, energetic woman and was deeply in love with her husband. When she returned from that shop, she began aging right in front of our eyes. It was incredibly unbelievable. So how do you account for her aging process?"

I shrugged my shoulders because I really didn't have an answer that would satisfy her. But I did my best and said, "I don't know what to tell you about that. I am not a medical doctor. I would guess that there was something medically wrong with her. Did she see any doctors about her disease?"

She nodded. "Yes, definitely. She sought out more doctors than you could count on your fingers."

"What did those doctors say?"

She shook her head in disgust, and said, "None of those so-called doctors of medicine could give her any feasible reason for what was causing her aging. Some thought it was in her genes."

"There you go. It's in her genes."

"But we didn't believe that. No one else in our family has had that particular problem. She even went to a few so-called specialists. But they couldn't solve her disease either. And after nearly a year of visiting doctor's offices, she finally gave up."

"So what did she do after that?"

"She started praying at her church," she replied matter-of-factly. "Remember, she has Gypsy blood running through her veins."

"So what does that mean?"

"She is very stubborn and hard headed. When she sets her mind to do something, she lets nothing interfere with it. She felt that if she didn't do something very soon, she wouldn't be around much longer."

"Why did she think that?" I asked her.

"Why…? Because she continued to age at an alarmingly fast rate. Much faster than the normal person…wouldn't you say! Do you think she is still alive?"

"Well, I don't know. But if she had an accident while driving to that costume shop, we will definitely find her. Hopefully, before it's too late. But I promise you that I'll get to the bottom of this mystery."

"I hope so," she whined, drying her eyes with a hankie.

Then I reassured her, saying, "Don't worry, Debby. If she is alive, we'll get her back. But before you leave the station, please, leave your name, address and phone number and a photo of your sister. Then I'll contact you when and if I find out any information concerning your sister's disappearance."

"Okay, but what should I do in the mean time?"

I told her to go home and get some rest. "I'll call you as soon as I hear something. I'll also file a missing person's report and contact the other police agencies in the area. They'll drive along the main roads that lead to that town and check very carefully and thoroughly to see if there are any signs of an accident or mishap," I said, as I walked her to the front desk.

"Do you really think that's what happened to her?" she asked, chewing her fingernails.

"Well, I'm not sure. But if the car <u>has</u> gone off the road…it could be hidden in deep underbrush. If so, there may be some skid marks leading to the vehicle's whereabouts, which hopefully will lead us to your sister. But don't worry about anything. We'll find her."

I told her goodbye and then turned and walked back to my desk.

I didn't think I would be visiting that town until the end of the week. But right at this moment I didn't care…because it was past my lunchtime and that was my first priority. So I decided to drive over to Gabriele's, my favorite café, and have an early dinner.

After eating my delicious meal, I thought about visiting that costume shop to ask that hunchback a few more questions – for some odd reason I couldn't get him out of my mind – and I could search for Mrs. Dante's car on the way…but decided against it. Because I needed daylight to look for her car. And the other police agencies should be looking for it by that time too…because they wouldn't start their search until I had filed the report and they had received the information at their roll call. So I postponed my trip to the costume shop until the following morning.

While relaxing at the cafe I had a chance to sit back and put my thoughts into perspective…and to focus my mind on the confusion of this puzzling case. To my regret, my mind became a clouded fog and my thoughts came together all at once. I had to quit thinking about this investigation because my head felt like it was going to explode into a billion pieces.

So I left the cafe and drove back to the station. But once there, I suddenly lost all my energy…and needed to get to my desk quickly and sit down or my knees would have buckled out from under me. Something weird was going on in my body. Just then I thought about Mrs. Dante…and that maybe I had caught her disease. But then I realized that I was becoming just a bit too paranoid. I was feeling ill because of my hangover, not because of some crazy disease that some demented, old woman had given me.

But whatever the reason, sweat began pouring off my forehead while I sat doubled over in my chair…feeling nauseated and dizzy. Maybe I had a case of food poisoning, I thought to myself? But within a few minutes, I was back to normal. Or so I thought.

I got out my partner's notebook and began looking through his case files, going through each one very thoroughly. Nothing caught my eye until I came to the fifth report, which I couldn't quite comprehend. Because it was written in his awful handwriting and hard to follow…and his sentence structure seemed out of context. But after reading four out of the five pages of the report I was able to put the pieces together. And I couldn't believe what I had just read. My missing partner had found many abnormal atrocities. Although he didn't elaborate, he did write that he was afraid of telling anyone his true theory on his most puzzling case. Because he thought he would be the butt of their jokes…even though he wanted to tell the whole world what he really thought of his investigation. But fear of being rejected by his peers…seemed to be the main motive of keeping quiet.

I had to read between the lines, but I was getting his message loud and clear. And the main word that he had underlined was <u>Legend</u>. I wondered if he was referring to the "Legend of Hollow Pass"…a story of historic proportions…and one that I knew little about. But would <u>soon</u> learn.

He also had written in his notebook that he regretted not revealing his answers to the many questions that came his way…and that keeping silent had been eating him up inside. So much so that he thought his head was gonna explode. The truth kept gnawing at him…because he had lied to the victim's wife, saying that her husband had probably run away with another woman to start life anew – the same thing Mrs. Dante was told – so he could close the case. But I don't think he really believed that…even though he didn't elaborate.

The end of the report states how my missing partner wanted to try out his theory on himself before he was consumed with ulcers or died of a heart attack. He mentioned how the case had taken its toll on his mind and body and had made him look ten years older.

Now that I think back, I did notice something strange about his outward appearance. His hair had turned gray…and practically overnight. In fact, many of the other detectives had noticed it too and had kidded him about it. He laughed it off, but you could tell it bothered him. Although I do recall that he did have a few bad days. And he had the flu or flu-like symptoms for almost two weeks straight. Heck, at the time I didn't think anything about it. But now that I think back on it, maybe it was the aging disease at work?

That made me question my own plight. It's all in my mind, I thought. There's nothing wrong with me that a good stiff drink couldn't fix. Alcohol killed any germs that infiltrated my body. So I wasn't worried. In fact, it was getting close to drinking time now. And all I wanted do…was go home and think about my partner's report… while cleaning out my innards with a few double shots of scotch.

But I had one last thing to do before leaving for home. I had to stop by the front desk and pick up the picture of Mrs. Dante, the lady in question. But when I did, I noticed one problem with it. The photo – with Debby's address and phone number written on the back of it – was of the woman at thirty-six, before the disease ravaged her body, and not as she looked now. This picture was of no use to me. I needed a recent one of her. Mrs. Dante's sister would have to fax me one … Pronto.

I needed to telephone Debby immediately. So I walked back to my desk and punched in her telephone number. She answered it after two rings.

"Hello," she said.

"Hello, Mrs. Charles, I mean, Debby. This is Detective Zoolu. I'm sorry to disturb you, but I'm calling to get a recent picture of your sister."

"I left you one, didn't you get it?"

"Yes. But it's of no use to me."

"Why is that?"

"This photo was taken when she was a beautiful, young woman. When I show the picture around, they need to see the real thing. Do you think you can fax me a recent photo of your sister?"

"I might have one somewhere around the house. But right off hand, I don't know where it is. As soon as I hang up the phone, I'll look for it and fax it over to you as soon as I find it."

"Thank you. I appreciate it," I said, giving her the fax number again before hanging up the phone.

I sat back and waited for the photo to come through the fax machine…until well past quitting time. I was just about ready to leave for home when the photo finally came through the fax machine. It was the picture I needed, showing the victim's face and body – an eighty-year-old face and body. I then placed the picture into my partner's notebook and left for home.

By the time I got there, I needed a large, stiff drink…because the traffic was horrendous. And between the traffic jams and this case, I was ready to explode. So a drink would calm my nerves. And that's exactly what I had as soon as I entered my home.

This case was beginning to take its toll on me. And I began making excuses for my odd behavior and excessive drinking – I was overtired, I had a hangover, I was too paranoid, I was stressed out… Anything to take a drink. But I didn't want to get too blasted tonight because I needed to be fresh and on my toes in the morning…for my drive out to that strange town…and especially if I wanted to outwit that cagey, hunchbacked, old man at the costume shop.

Because…by the time I arrived there, especially after experiencing Mother Nature's anger at Devil's Mountain, I was a bundle of nerves. My body would be shaking so badly that I would have to shut my eyes and take three or four deep breaths to calm myself down.

So I would keep my drinking to a minimum tonight. And I did, at first.

I had only two double shots while reading my missing partner's case file.

Although my partner didn't exactly write down what had happened to his victim, he tried to explain his thoughts without sounding like a fruitcake…especially when writing about driving up a mountainous road and experiencing unexplained weather conditions that seemed to come out of nowhere – such as eerie, gusting winds that had nearly blown his car off the road, hail as big as pool balls coming down from big, black, stormy clouds that seemed to swallow up his car, fog so thick that he couldn't see a foot in front of his face and gigantic lightning bolts – which was something that I hadn't experienced yet…and hoped not to!

He also had written about something that had taken control of his car, mind and body during his car ride in the mountains…and when he tried to fight it, the invisible force became even stronger. He was at its mercy…and a beaten man.

That's why, after experiencing this strange phenomenon, he was afraid to write a report about it, not wanting to seem like an odd ball. And that's why his investigation was eating him up inside. He had to keep it secret…and couldn't say what was really on his mind.

But I didn't see anything written concerning <u>my</u> theory. I believed that that old man, Jackson Billing was somehow doing away with his customers, then selling off the automobiles and any valuables that they might have had. And once that was accomplished, he and his partners probably buried the bodies out in that desert somewhere.

The only theory that was explained in the file was about the guy leaving town with another woman and starting a new life somewhere else. There was another, however, but it was written in some sort of code…which needed to be deciphered before I could find out what my partner had meant when he wrote…that he wanted to "try it" himself. Exactly what he meant by "try it," I wasn't certain?

I didn't see any mention about a time warp or any reference to a sorcerer. Although it still seemed he was referring to something sinister.

Now it was my turn to find out where these people were disappearing to…and why?

My thirst finally got the best of me and I began pouring drink after drink down my gullet while thinking about my investigation…and trying to drown my theories into oblivion.

Well, I had planned not to drink too much tonight. But that plan went out the window when I tried to bury my unanswered questions in my booze. And it worked too – that is until I passed out on my couch…with the scotch bottle still clutched in my hand. And I woke up with a terrible hangover, not spry and energetic like I had planned – just the opposite. My drinking had become a bad habit of late. But at least I didn't have any nightmares…that I could remember anyway.

I had to take a cold shower to sharpen my senses. Then, after dressing, went into the kitchen where I ate a couple of soft-boiled eggs and washed them down with a few cups of hot, black coffee. Minutes later, I grabbed my coat and my partner's notebook and headed out the door for work. But because of my massive hangover, I decided not to visit that crazy costume shop this morning. Instead, I would question Detective Matthew's witness.

Ten minutes later, I was sitting at my desk with paper in hand – that contained the address and phone number of the witness in question. But Matthew hadn't written down the witness's name. I dialed the number anyway and waited for someone to answer.

"Northville Mental Health Department," said the woman on the other end of the phone.

"Hello, I'm Detective Zoolu from the city police department," I said, very surprised to have reached a mental institution.

"What can I do for you, detective?"

"I seem to have a problem. I'm not real sure who I want to speak with. I wonder, is there a way to find out who Detective Matthew visited when he was there a couple of days, or maybe even a week ago?" I asked, hoping the woman would take the time to help me out.

"Well, hold on a minute and I will look at the sign-in-sheet. You said his name was Detective what?"

"His name is Detective John Matthew."

"And you said he might have visited up to a week ago. Is that right?"

"Yes. Do you see his name anywhere?"

"One minute please," she said, looking at her sign-in sheet. "Yes, here it is. He was here on the twenty-third. That was three days ago. He visited a Mrs. Irene Kall."

"You said her name was Kall. K-A-L-L?" I asked.

"Yes. She is on the third floor in ward B."

"What is ward B?"

She hesitated for a moment, then said, "Those people on that floor are in bad shape. If you want to talk to her, you should visit her early in the morning, before she gets dosed."

"Why is that?"

"She is on some heavy medication and isn't coherent most of the day."

"Has she been dosed yet?"

"I believe she has. If not yet, she will be…within a few more minutes. But it still takes about fifteen minutes before the medication kicks in."

"Why is she in the nut house?" I asked, wanting to know the answer.

"I'm sorry, I can't give out that information. I've said too much already."

"Well I probably won't be able to see her today. So I'll visit her tomorrow morning…before she takes her medication. I need to ask her a few questions. But I thank you for your time. You've been very helpful. Thanks again. Bye, Bye," I said, then hung up the phone.

Well no wonder Detective Matthew wanted me to question his witness. She's in the nut house. He probably arrived there too late, after she had already been medicated. Or he didn't get any answers to his questions?

Either way, he still wanted me to listen to her story...even though she's probably too stoned to answer any questions sensibly.

Evidently, Matthew just wanted me to do his dirty work. Well, that's all right, I thought. It may help me in my investigation.

CHAPTER 5

Well, it was just about lunchtime when I had finished speaking to the receptionist at the nut house, so I decided to get some food "to go" from Gabriele's.

Then I was going to ride out to the costume shop and ask that funny-looking, hunchback, Jackson Billing, a few tough questions. And when my questioning was completed, I would drive back to the station and hope I had enough evidence against him to convince a judge to sign a search warrant…so I would have the legal authority to search the old man's mysterious, costume shop and surrounding area.

And, if by chance I should run into that mysterious weather again at Devil's mountain, then, most likely, I would also run into that invisible force. But before I did I wanted to try out my theory – which was to drink myself into a drunken stupor and hope, by doing that…would neutralize that invisible force from controlling my body and mind?

If I had told any of my co-workers or superiors about this phenomenon, they would have laughed me into the funny farm. And I would have been tossed off this investigation immediately if I had mentioned any of the crazy happenings that I had experienced and encountered. So I wasn't going to take a chance and ruin my reputation and employment. And without a witness or witnesses to back me up, I would do as my partner had and not mention anything about these mysterious forces until I had positive proof to back up my words.

On my way to the costume shop, just after two o'clock in the afternoon, I finally ate my hoagie sandwiches. That sure hit the spot…and settled my stomach.

It took me a good two hours of hard driving to reach Devil's Mountain. Again, the mountainous area just suddenly appeared out of nowhere while the main road that I had been driving on had disappeared just as fast.

And as I climbed that treacherous, mountainous, dirt road, the weather turned for the worse – again…and by the time I had reached the peak of the mountain, the horrible weather turned into a devil's torment as the dark, rumbling clouds and thick fog surrounded my car while the wind began shaking it…and then, seconds later, tossing it from one side of the road to the other…bringing me to the edge of the ravine before whipping me back to the other side, within inches of the mountain.

Gathering my senses, I decided to try out my theory before that invisible force took control of my mind. But it was too late…because just at that moment, I felt that invisible force take control of my body. I tried to reach for my bottle of scotch, but I was frozen to the seat…and couldn't move a muscle. But even if I could, I had forgotten to bring the bottle of scotch with me, so I would have to try out my theory another time – to see if a drunken stupor could stop that mysterious, invisible force from zapping my energy from my body and mind.

I tried to fight back as the car followed the winding, dirt road down the mysterious mountain but the force was much too strong. And the harder I fought it, the stronger the force became. I even tried to pinch myself to see if I was dreaming, but I couldn't. My hands were frozen to the steering wheel. And that's when I realized…I wasn't dreaming…and couldn't do anything about it even if I was.

I finally regained control of my faculties just as the car reached the bottom of the mountain. But before driving any further, I had to take a few deep breaths and gather my senses. And after a couple of minutes of meditation, I was ready to start my drive towards the town. But just as I pressed down on the accelerator I noticed, about a hundred feet in front of me, a very tall and huge figure walking along the side of the road towards town. I thought it was a Bigfoot creature.

But as I came upon this strapping figure of a large being, it suddenly turned towards my car and stuck out its thumb, as though it was hitchhiking and begging for a ride into town. That's when I knew that it wasn't a Bigfoot at all…but a huge, huge man wearing a large bearskin coat.

As I stopped the car to ask him if he wanted a ride, I wondered if this was the same person that I had seen walking in the opposite direction a few days before.

I motioned for him to open the passenger door.

"Do you want a ride?" I asked the hitchhiker as he bent down and opened the passenger door, sticking his head inside the car.

But he didn't answer me and just stared into my eyes. As our silence grew, I noticed the big man was carrying a small, wrapped package under his right arm, holding onto it very tightly as though it contained something of value. I was going to ask him about it but I didn't want to stick my nose where it didn't belong. And I sure didn't want to upset him…because this man was huge. He was an old Indian man, probably in his seventies or eighties. And had to be a good seven and a half feet tall while probably weighing in at a good four hundred and fifty pounds, with a neck that stretched to a foot long. He was as *big* as a grizzly bear. And had a weathered, wrinkled face, a big, bulbous nose and long, white hair that fell to his waist. He looked as though he had come out of a fairy tale…and was definitely, a giant of a man.

Finally, after a long minute of silence, he accepted my invitation with a nod. He had a little trouble entering the car, though. I moved the seat as far back as I could, so he could sit in the car without being all scrunched up. But even so, his head hit the top of the roof and his bent knees came up to the windshield. He was a massive sight. There was nothing more I could do to help him; he was as comfortable as he was going to get. He was just too darn big.

Once he had shut his door, I continued my drive towards the town.

"Thank you for the ride," said the monstrous Indian placing his bundle in his scrunched up lap. "Are you going into town?"

Jokingly, I looked around to see if there was any other place for me to visit, then answered, "Yep, that's where I'm headed. Where are you going?"

"I'm going to the Costume shop to sell a costume."

"How often do you visit that place?" I asked him.

"Now, about two or three times a year…instead of three or four times a month like I used to years ago…because my body is getting too old to walk the distance from my little village."

"How far do you live from town?"

"About five miles. … I'm not as young as I used to be. Now, Mother Nature and I fight for survival."

"Fight for survival. What do you mean?" I asked him.

"She is trying to keep me away. And I fight to come here."

"Who wins?"

"In my younger days the fight was short. I won easily. But now, she is much stronger and tougher than I am. It is a much longer battle these days, but I still manage to break through. But soon, old Mother Nature will overpower my senses and I will lose the battle. But I will continue until my body can no longer make the sacrifice."

I didn't really know what he was talking about? But I let him ramble on.

"Who are you visiting out here?" I asked.

"I came to see the same person you are here to see."

"Who is that?"

"The costume man, of course," said the mysterious, old Indian man, smiling, exposing the few teeth left in his mouth.

"How did you know that?"

"I know many things. Some say I have a third eye. But his shop is the only business around here."

"You're right about that. The rest of the town is deserted."

"It is now. But it used to be a booming mining town. When the silver mine went bust, so did the town. Soon after, many of the townspeople died from some sickness. Only a few of the hard core, townsfolk stayed. But there are many lost souls that stayed behind. Many lost souls," he said, mysteriously.

"Why do you want to see the old man at the costume shop?" I asked him.

"I have something he wants," replied the old Indian, patting the wrapped bundle sitting on his lap.

Wanting to find out what he knew about Jackson Billing, I decided that the best way to get this strange man to open up was to befriend him. And the best way to do that, I figured, was to converse with him on a name to name basis. So I introduced myself, saying, "I'm sorry...I forgot to introduce myself. I'm Brad Zoolu. What's your name, if you don't mind me asking?"

"They call me Wallahoo Cecil. I'm glad to meet you." We shook hands.

And now that we were friends, I asked him the question that was on my mind–concerning Jackson Billing. "How long have you known Jackson Billing, the costume shop owner? What do you know about him?"

But he suddenly froze up, his face turning white as a ghost. "I'm sorry," he said, cautiously looking around as if he was going to get struck by a bolt of lightning. "I've talked too much already."

"What are you afraid of?"

"Please," he pleaded, grabbing my shoulder and looking me in the eyes, "you must go and not come back here."

"Why? What are you talking about?"

He took his hand from my shoulder, bowed his head and said, "This town will eat you alive. It will swallow you whole and spit you out. Please leave. Danger lurks in the shadows."

"Well, sir," I retorted, "I don't scare that easily. I have been protecting the public for over twenty-five years. I'm not about to stop now."

"Why is that? Are you a blue coat?"

I didn't know what the hell he was talking about so I asked him, "A blue coat? What's that?"

He gave me a surprise look and exclaimed, "You know, a soldier."

I just laughed, saying, "Do I look like a soldier?"

He shook his head, no.

"You're right. I'm not a soldier. I'm a homicide detective. And I think I can take care of myself."

"No one can fight the Indian spirits, Mr. Zoolu. They say this area is a very old, Indian burial ground. As old as earth itself. There are many evil spirits that roam this area."

"Why is that?"

His answer sent shivers down my spine.

"The evil souls were buried here. Not the good souls. Only the evil ones."

But I didn't believe in all that mumbo jumbo. "I'm just not superstitious," I told him.

But my words fell on deaf ears.

"Sometimes," he replied, "it is smart to be superstitious."

To change the subject, I asked him again to tell me what he knew about Jackson Billing.

But he didn't answer right away. In fact, for nearly a minute there was a deathly silence in the car. Only a loud heartbeat could be heard – coming from the old mysterious Indian.

Just as I was about to speak up, he said, "The gods will throw their vengeance upon me for giving away their secrets. But, I will tell you what I have heard. My ancestors told me about that hunchbacked, old man when I was a little boy. He was an old man at that time."

But that just didn't make sense. And I told him so. "How could he be an old man when you were a young boy? He must be well into his seventies. And you look about the same age?"

He shook his head, saying, "He's much older."

"I don't believe it. That's impossible."

But Wallahoo told me more. "My grandfather also knew of him, when he was a boy."

"I don't believe that either."

"I was also told by my grandfather…that his grandfather had told him too about an old, hunchback, little man with bulging eyes that worked in a costume shop. But he wasn't a man at all. He was really the Devil in disguise."

"I think you're pulling my leg, Wallahoo," I snickered.

He added, "Your family must have lived in this area during the War of the States."

"Are you talking about the Civil War?" I asked, scratching my head. He nodded. "Well, you're right. My ancestors did live here during that time period. Why?"

"You wouldn't be here now, if you weren't related to someone who had lived in this area more than a century ago."

But I didn't know what the hell he was talking about. And told him so.

"What the hell are you talking about?" I barked.

But just as I was about to question him further on it, we arrived in front of the costume shop. So my questions would have to wait.

And so would my interview with Jackson Billing…because as we hopped out of the car I noticed that there was a sign on the shop's door saying it was "closed."

I couldn't believe it. It never had crossed my mind that the shop would be closed. Boy, this was really a big letdown for me. Now, I would have to turn around and head back to the office. What a wasted trip, I thought to myself.

"Wallahoo, can I give you a lift back, seeing the shop is closed?"

"No, I will walk to my friend's house just up the street," he said, pointing a finger in the direction he was going.

I looked in the direction that he had pointed to see if there were any houses in that area. But I didn't see nothing but desert. That was it. Only cactus and tumbleweeds.

I decided to knock on the costume shop door anyway hoping someone would answer it. But when I didn't get any reaction from inside, I turned to speak to the old Indian. I wanted to ask him where his friend's house was. But when I turned around, he was nowhere in sight. I couldn't believe my eyes. He had disappeared in a flash. My eyes searched the empty town but Wallahoo was nowhere to be found.

I wondered if I was dreaming or if any of this was really happening? Was that old Indian just a figment of my imagination or ... A mirage?

This place was beginning to drive me crazy. I didn't know what was real and what wasn't real anymore.

I was confused, disoriented and very disenchanted, having to leave empty-handed. However, this trip wasn't a total waste of time. I did find out some information. Whether it was pertinent to the investigation or not, was still undetermined.

I jumped back into my car and headed for the station. As I slowly drove away from the town, looking into my rear-view mirror I noticed a small boy in the background. I wished I had seen him a few minutes earlier. I could have asked him a few questions. Like, did he know why the shop was closed?

But instead, I decided to save the questions for another day. Because I had decided to visit the woman at the nuthouse – that is, if it wasn't too late by the time I had returned to the city. Most likely though, I'd put it off until the following morning.

I just hoped I felt better. I figured I was coming down with something. Either a cold or the flu, or maybe both.

As I was leaving the deserted city, I couldn't stop thinking about what that old Indian man, Wallahoo Cecil, had told me. About how this place was an old Indian burial grounds and full of Indian spirits. I couldn't get that out of my mind.

And then, just as I reached Devil's Mountain, I began thinking about what I wanted to do next in my investigation. A few minutes before, I had decided to visit the woman at the nuthouse…but now I decided to go to the library first, and find out the history of Devil's Mountain. That is, if they had any history books on it.

While in deep thought, I began feeling that invisible force upon me once again. And as I started up the winding, mountain road, I experienced those same sensations and weather conditions that I had experienced and fought with before – strong, howling winds and a thick fog that blackened the sky and blinded my sense of direction. I tried to press down on the accelerator but my body was totally paralyzed by that evil force.

Suddenly those howling, rough winds began to push my car faster and faster up the mountain road, tossing it to and fro until I became so frightened I thought I would lose my bladder. But that invisible force had control of that, too.

When I thought things couldn't get any worse, the skies opened up and began dropping buckets of rain and hail, all the while my car swerving from one side of the road to the other. I wondered if it would ever end.

But then, as I descended the mountain, Mother Nature's rage finally seemed to relax. The fog dissipated and the rains and hail evaporated. Finally, after what seemed like all of eternity, I again had control of the car and myself.

This place was definitely strange. Thank God I was finally out of that weird, mysterious area and heading towards <u>my</u> town.

But I would return there soon. And keep an eye open for that old Indian man. I still wanted to ask him a few more questions…especially about that hunchback, Jackson Billing? But would he tell me anything? Because he seemed awful frightened of something – like offending his gods.

I had all kinds of questions running through my clouded mind that I wanted and needed answered. They wouldn't go away. My mind was being overloaded with troubled questions and evil thoughts. So much so, that I was still dazed and confused by the time I arrived back in the city.

Even with such a clouded mind, I did remember, however, to stop by the library to pick up a few history books.

After parking the car, I strolled into the building of books. It had been many, many years since I had visited the library. It took me a little while to find the books I needed, but after searching for an hour I finally found what I was looking for...and signed out a total of three books. One went back as far as the early eighteen hundreds.

With that chore completed, I then drove back to the station with my newly acquired books in hand. I walked directly to my desk and began looking through them. Two of the books didn't give me much information. Not what I was looking for, anyway. But the third book, the one that went back to the early eighteen hundreds, told a story about the first settlers that came to the area in question. They were met by a tribe of Indians. But this wasn't exactly the everyday Indian tribe. This was a tribe of witch doctors. They believed in the evil spirits...and were always conjuring them up while dancing to a full moon.

Many of the new settlers had seen strange things happening...and had become frightened of their Indian neighbors. So the settlers began killing them off, one by one, until they were all dead, and their tribe had become extinct. But before the last one died, he conjured up all the evil spirits in the universe and put an evil curse on their town...or so the story goes. This was the "Legend of Hollow Pass."

The Indians could never bury their dead because some of the townsfolk had dismembered their bodies and sold the meat to unsuspecting cowboys, ranch hands and others. The ravaged, Indian souls were still roaming the earth because they were never given to the gods.

The book showed a picture of the store and restaurant and its owner, who had supposedly sold the meat in question during the eighteen sixties. The closer I looked at that picture, the more I noticed that the old man in the picture sure looked like Jackson Billing, the hunchback, old man from the costume shop. No, it couldn't be, I thought.

I made photocopies of the pictures – to have them blown up and then compare the old man in the photo to the old man from the costume shop.

I finished reading about the history of the town and its occupants, but one paragraph caught my attention and stuck in my mind. It stated that the town disappeared into oblivion when all of its townspeople died from the plague, which many believed was due to the evil Indian's curse against them.

People from the surrounding towns supposedly burned down the diseased town and then hired a preacher to exorcise the grounds where the town once stood. From that day forward, it was known as a ghost town. That's when the "Legend of Hollow Pass" began.

Then it hit me! If the town had burned down over a hundred and thirty years ago, what is it doing there now? I had become so overloaded with mind-boggling questions concerning that town, its people and the costume shop that I had gotten a headache.

So I tried to take my mind off of that place and think about what my next step would be in my investigation. But I still couldn't think clearly. So I left the station and drove back to the library. I returned the books to the assistant, then left…for parts unknown.

I jumped back into my car, but hadn't decided what I wanted to do next. I was very anxious to visit the lady at the nuthouse…to interview her and hear her story. But it would have to wait until morning. Right now my shift was over…and I was ready to go home. I desperately needed a break away from this case. It was literally driving me crazy.

So much so, that my gray hairs had more than doubled – what few I had left, that is. And my face had wrinkles where before I had none. My walk had become slower and my posture…much worse. In fact, I couldn't straighten up any more. I was slowly becoming a hunchback like Jackson Billing. And there wasn't much I could do about it.

I blamed my physical ailments on stress and exhaustion. And worrying about it didn't help either. So I just pushed it out of my mind. Or I tried to anyway.

Tonight I just wanted to relax, get drunk and forget all my troubles.

I drove straight home. I wanted to stop at my favorite cafe for hoagies but I wanted to have a drink even more…and was sitting in my living room with a bottle of scotch in hand within ten minutes.

I tried not thinking about my strange case, but it wouldn't leave my conscious mind. Especially after seeing a picture of a man that was taken back in Civil War time and seemed to still be alive. I didn't know what to think?

But that wasn't the only strange thing that had occurred. Now I was growing old before my eyes – at about the same rate as a dog.

After finishing a full liter bottle of liquid dreams – lately it's been a bottle of nightmares – I passed out on the couch. Around three o'clock in the morning though, I had awakened from that horrifying nightmare, remembering everything that I had dreamt about.

This time though, I asked the hunchback at the costume shop if he was the reason that people were disappearing after visiting his shop. Suddenly his face distorted into a hideous, monstrous shape twice its normal size that included a grotesque, big-lipped mouth that spewed fire rings. His hands doubled in size, while blisters and puss-filled boils popped out all over his scaly skin.

The hunchback stayed behind his counter, as if it protected him from some evil spirit. I teased him to come out and get me like a man. But he just cowered down behind his counter and spit fire rings and small fireballs at me. Most of them, however, lost their flame before they made contact.

I continued to antagonize this strange, little fat man hoping he would come out from behind his counter. But he refused and stayed in his little domain. I thought I had the upper hand, until he began laughing and then inhaled my body in one swallow.

Just as I felt my body being digested in the pit of this evil hunchback's stomach, I awoke in a sopping sweat and out of breath. I guess he showed me who was boss, I thought to myself.

I tried to fall back to sleep but I just tossed and turned the rest of the night. Actually, I was afraid to go back to sleep, not wanting to have that terrible nightmare again…because I might not wake up – for the simple reason of being swallowed alive.

I also noticed in my nightmare that the hunchback never came out from behind the counter. It's as though the rules of the shop wouldn't allow it.

Every time I've had this nightmare, I wake up and I'm never able to get back to sleep. This time, I just stayed up and drank many cups of hot, black coffee. It didn't get rid of my pounding headache, but it sure gave me plenty of energy.

After I finished the first pot of coffee, I jumped into the shower. I washed, shaved and dressed with plenty of time to spare before I had to leave for work. This was a first for me. Usually, I'm so hung over from the partying and drinking I had done the night before, that I had absolutely no energy and my stomach screamed for help. Most days, I can't see clearly and my eyes are puffy and bloodshot. But not today. I was awake, alert, and roaring to go. And ready for my visit to the nuthouse, to interview Detective Matthew's eyewitness.

But first I had to visit the station. Once I had signed in, I then went to my desk to retrieve a few items that I would need for the interview. Ten minutes later, I was on my way to see the woman that had an experience at the shop and ended up at the mental hospital. She had not only lost her husband, but also her mind.

To get there, I had to drive to the outskirts of the city on the south side of town. And by the time I had arrived I felt older than the hospital, which was built at the turn of the century. Giant, weeping willow trees surrounded the old, dilapidated, red, brick building. And rows of them adorned both sides of the sidewalk, leading all the way to the front doors.

There was definitely an eeriness about this place. Grotesque and evil-looking gargoyles – which seemed to watch ones' every move – adorned all four corners of the red brick building.

And as I walked towards the nuthouse, the weather seemed to change to a windless cold. Even though it was summertime and the sun was shining, the cold air went right through my body, until I began shivering and couldn't stop. And the closer I came to the building, the colder it got…and my shivering became unbearable. In fact, my teeth chattered so much I thought they would break off.

But once I had entered the building, my body suddenly warmed up; it seemed to be on fire…and my sight was affected, as if something had warped my vision.

Everything seemed to be floating, as if I was underwater and in slow motion. It felt as though I had inhaled some type of hallucinogenic drug. Because my head felt as though it was going to drop from my shoulders. And I had a sudden bout of dizziness, lightheadedness and hot flashes.

As I looked around, I noticed that this place wasn't a hospital, but a prison. The inside of this huge, old building contained only one giant room. And all four sides of the room were sectioned off in tiers. One tier on top of the other. Just like the cellblocks in prison, except they had completely enclosed rooms for these inmates. Instead of barred cells, there were twenty, small, padded rooms to each side, and their doors made of solid, four inch, thick steel…which included – about five feet from the ground – a small, three inch, square glass window to look through, and beneath that, a thin slit to pass the food tray in and out.

The rooms were only six-foot square with a seven-foot high ceiling – smaller than a monkey cage at the zoo – with three-inch thick, padded mats surrounding all four walls and some having padded floors. But no blanket or pillow, no sink or toilet, no mirror or television, just four bland, white, padded walls. The only other item in the room besides the patient was a metal bedpan. It was supposed to be a sterile type room. What a joke!

Most patients were forced to wear straightjackets so they couldn't harm or mutilate themselves. Whew. After looking at this place, if the patient wasn't crazy when they arrived here, they sure would be when they left. Staying locked up in a room like that would drive anyone crazy.

A staff member (nurse) escorted me to the young lady's room that I was interested in interviewing. It was at the far end of the building and on the seventh tier. The tiers were in chronological order. The first floor is for the sanest patients…with the eighth tier being for the most insane and the most destructive.

The nurse revealed that the female patient I wanted to interview had been here for over two years. She hadn't improved at all, only deteriorated – and was labeled insane and manic-depressive by the psychiatric staff after she told them her story about her husband being devoured by lions in a gladiator pit during the time of Caesar and the Roman Empire.

We arrived at the room before the nurse was able to finish the story about the patient. I looked through the little, glass window and watched the patient's reaction as the nurse unlocked the heavy, steel door so I could interview her from inside the little room.

The female, mental patient – wearing a straightjacket – was balled up in the far corner of the room, facing the wall and mumbling to herself. Her bedclothes were very dirty and stained with urine and fecal matter.

As I entered the room, she didn't even notice me. Her long, thin, dirty, white hair was all I could see of her. When she turned around towards me, I was quite startled and shocked at what I was looking at. This woman was supposed to be a young lady. She had just turned twenty-four years of age, two months before, but she looked like an old, sickly lady of eighty or ninety. Her teeth – the few that she had in her mouth – were a yellowish-green and black color. They looked as though they were rotting away, right in front of my eyes. Her eye sockets were sunken and drawn; her face, gaunt and anorexic looking. She looked like she was slowly dying from malnutrition and neglect, a skeleton…just skin and bones. I felt very sorry for her. And nearly left the room without asking her anything.

I wanted the woman to open up during our interview…and to do that she would have to feel comfortable. So I asked the nurse to undo the woman's straightjacket, but my request was denied.

I shrugged my shoulders and turned to the patient to begin my interview. But before I could ask her my first question, I had to take a few deep breaths to gather my strength.

"Mrs. Kall, hello. I'm Detective Zoolu. I want to talk to you about the disappearance of your husband. Do you understand me?" I asked her, as I looked deep into her teary, sunken, red eyes.

She just sat and stared as though she was in a drug-like trance, staring right through me. I didn't know if she had even heard me? She looked so lost and pitiful I was very saddened by her appearance and demeanor. Looking at her made me sick to my stomach, but I tried once again to talk with her.

"Do you hear me, Mrs. Kall? You do remember when your husband disappeared, don't you?" But she remained silent, and just sat frozen, balled up in a fetal position.

I was just about ready to give up and leave the room when she finally spoke to me.

"Yes, I remember when my husband disappeared…and yes, I hear you," she replied, slobbering on herself and slurring her words as she spoke. "Why are you interested in his disappearance now? The police department wasn't interested in it two years ago."

"Why is that, Mrs. Kall?"

She gave me a dirty look and replied, "They all thought I was crazy. They still think I'm crazy. Look at me…I tell them the truth and they put me in a straightjacket. They think I'm an embarrassment to the human race, so they hide me in here and forget about me. Why should I talk with you at all?"

I pleaded with her. "Please, I'm trying to help you. I want to know everything that you saw that day your husband disappeared."

But she didn't think I would believe a "crazy woman".

I told her I would, adding, "I promise not to interrupt."

After a long pause, she began telling me her story. "My husband and I went to visit my sister to see the new home she had just built. We were going to plan a Halloween party that she had been thinking of throwing. But somehow we got turned around halfway through the trip. We were on the main thoroughfare and then suddenly, out of nowhere, a large dark cloud surrounded our car and we found ourselves driving up a mountain road."

"Why didn't you turn around when you saw that you were lost?" I asked her.

She shrugged her shoulders. "We didn't know where we were. The picturesque scenery had suddenly changed into mountainous terrain. Then we ran into a windstorm and a very foggy haze. The fog blinded us. We had to slow down to nearly a crawl. Even then the wind nearly picked the car up and pitched it over the edge of the cliff into a rocky ravine two thousand feet below. We both nearly defecated in our pants…like I do now."

"What happened next?" I asked.

She continued: "Something very strange happened. Some evil spirit took control of our bodies and our minds. My husband even lost control of the vehicle. We tried to fight whatever it was controlling us, but it was totally useless."

They had experienced the same phenomenon as I had. So I asked her, "How long did that last?"

She shrugged her shoulders and replied, "I'm not sure. When we finally broke out of that weird storm, we were on the floor of the canyon. That's when the force that had control of us finally relinquished its hold."

"So why, Mrs. Kall, didn't you turn around and go back the way you came once you had control of your car and faculties, as you say happened?"

"Because my husband noticed the car was low on fuel and saw a town a few hundred yards ahead of us. So we drove there to see if we could buy gas and ask directions to my sister's address."

"Did you?"

"Well...when we arrived in that little town, we didn't see any gas station, but we did notice a cute, little, wooden building called the Costume Shop. We were going to my sister's costume party in three days and needed costumes. So we decided to visit the shop."

"It was open then?"

She nodded yes, adding, "A little, hunchback, old man sitting behind the counter and dressed up in a joker's outfit was running it. And when he saw me, he gave me such a weird look that I got shivers all up and down my body."

"What did your husband do?"

"My husband didn't see my reaction. He was too interested in the beautiful costumes. Especially a gladiator costume."

"You have to be in good shape to wear a costume like that, don't you, Mrs. Kall?" I asked.

She nodded, adding, "My husband worked out at the gym nearly every day and looked great. He was really fit. He liked the costume and I agreed with him. So he tried it on in the changing room." As she spoke, she rocked back and forth while sitting on the dirty floor in one corner of the room.

"Mrs. Kall, what did you do while your husband was changing into his costume?"

"I found a costume for myself – a Cleopatra outfit. But I couldn't change into it because my husband was still using the changing room. So while I waited I read the rules of the store, which were posted on the wall directly behind the counter."

"What was that hunchback, old man doing while you were reading the sign?"

She gave me a strange look and replied, "Ogling my body."

"Are you sure? Maybe he was just admiring your body?"

She shook her head no. "I swear, he was drooling and slobbering all over himself. It was disgusting. I think he was actually trying to flirt with me."

"So, what did you do?"

"I just ignored his actions. And when my husband came out of the changing room wearing his costume, I went and tried mine on."

"Do you know when he disappeared?"

She thought for a few seconds, and then answered, "Just before I walked into the changing room. My husband told me he was going out to the car to put his clothes away. Just as he opened the front door of the shop I turned to walk into the changing room. All of a sudden, out of the corner of my eye, I saw a glimpse of a bright flash of light and then at that very same moment, I heard the roar of a large crowd."

"So, what did you do?"

"What do you think I did? I turned and ran towards the open door."

"What did you see, Mrs. Kall?"

But she remained silent.

So, I asked her again, "Please, tell me what you saw."

After a little more coaxing, she finally answered, "I saw a big Roman or Greek coliseum…that had pits of fire, lions and tigers and dead gladiators. And some of those dead gladiators were being eaten by the lions and tigers."

"What did you do?" I asked her, anxiously waiting to hear the answer.

"What could I do? I rushed to the door. And saw a giant lion jump straight at me. But it hit the doorjamb instead. When he slammed into it, the door slammed into me, knocking me back, and then it closed shut."

"What happened to you? Were you hurt?" I asked her.

"I think I must have fainted, but I'm not sure. I was very upset and confused."

"Was that the last time you saw your husband?"

She looked down at the floor and nodded. "When I stood up and opened the door, the landscape was just like it was when we first arrived. The lions, tigers and gladiators were gone. And so was my husband…along with the car that we rode in. Then, I guess I fainted."

"What happened when you woke up?"

Spitting through her rotten teeth as she spoke, she snapped, "I was in a straightjacket and in this nuthouse."

"Mrs. Kall, let me see if I understand you correctly. You say you saw lions, tigers, gladiators and fire pits in an arena?"

"Yes," she replied, rocking back and forth.

"Do you know if Caesar was emperor at that time?" I asked jokingly, and let out a little laugh over my senseless humor.

She gave me a dirty look. "Just as I thought," she grumbled. "You came here to ridicule me. Well, all of you, get out of here!"

I apologized for my remarks and idiotic behavior. "I'm sorry, Mrs. Kall. I didn't mean anything by my stupid remarks."

But she refused my apology and scolded me, "You're just like all the rest of them. I open my heart and tell you the truth and all you can do is crack jokes. I'm in a damn straightjacket. Does it look like I'm joking around?"

I again apologized for my remarks, adding, "You might think I'm crazy, but I believe you. I believe your story."

She reacted slowly to my words and then suddenly realized that I believed her. "You do?" she replied and sat up straight – as straight as she could under the circumstances – her face shining a sign of hope. "Can I ask you why you believe me?"

I told her that I also had some strange things happen to me in that area, adding, "But I would never tell my superiors that or I'd be in the room next to yours?"

"Can you get me out of this nuthouse?" she asked, as tears flowed from her eyes.

I didn't want to get her hopes up, but promised her, "I'm going to do whatever it takes to get to the bottom of this mystery. Too many people are disappearing and I know that costume shop owner has something to do with it. I'm sure of that. But I tend to think he's somehow drugging his customers with some type of hallucinogen, then robs and kills them, taking all their money and other valuables, and probably buries their bodies somewhere out in that vast desert surrounding his shop."

"Then go arrest him."

I told her I couldn't. "I need some hard evidence against him…that I can take to a judge, so he'll issue a search warrant for the shop's premises and surrounding area. I just can't go on rumor or hearsay. I have more investigating to do first."

"You better stop that crazy man or more people are going to disappear," Kall predicted.

I told her that I'd try, and then thanked her for the interview, adding, "I may come back one day and speak with you again? If that's okay with you?"

She told me to visit her anytime because she wasn't going anywhere, then gave me her opinion on her husband's disappearance. "I don't think that man from the costume shop killed anyone. I think an evil force or evil spirit is taking them for sacrificial lambs. They are payment for the extermination of the Indian tribe that once roamed that area during the last couple of centuries. Their evil spirits are still here on earth. Haven't you heard of the Legend of Hollow Pass?"

I snickered, then said, "Yes, I've heard of it and I'll look into it further. But now, I must be going. Take care of yourself."

But she had one more thing to say to me. "Before you leave, you may want to talk with the man on the floor above. I think his wife disappeared in the same fashion."

"Is that right, nurse? How long has he been here?" I asked.

But before the nurse could answer the question, Mrs. Kall answered for her. "He came here only ten or eleven months ago. His story is similar to mine. But he went plum loco after his experience at that costume shop."

"Mrs. Kall, do you know for a fact that he and his wife visited that costume shop when his wife disappeared?" I asked.

"That's what I hear."

"How do you know this if you're stuck in this room twenty-four hours a day?"

"I told you…he's right above my floor."

"So what?"

"These walls are hollow. When he's coherent, we talk to each other. Listen to his story, Detective. If you think mine is hard to believe, just listen to his," said Mrs. Kall, rocking back and forth on the dirty floor in her fetal position.

"I will, that is if the nurse will escort me to his room? I'll ask him if he's in the mood to speak with me. If he is, I'll gladly talk to him."

With that said, my interview with Mrs. Kall was finished. I walked out of the room and the nurse locked the door behind me. She then escorted me to the eighth floor – to another disturbed patient who was possibly a witness to my investigation.

I watched the patient's face as I looked through the little window in the door. He also was in a straightjacket. And my initial reaction was dismay and helplessness. His appearance and mental state seemed worse than Mrs. Kall's.

"Nurse, what's this patient's name?" I asked her.

She replied, "Mr. Saber, Mr. Donald Saber."

The nurse slowly opened the door. She went in first and I followed. Saber was in a far corner, all curled up in a tight ball and facing the wall. When he turned to look at us, his face suddenly distorted into a beastly demon. Then, without warning, he leapt off the floor and butted me in the stomach with his head, knocking me against the wall behind me.

While I was trying to get up off the floor, the patient suddenly attacked the nurse. But within seconds, three large, male attendants burst into the room and took control of the situation and the patient. After a few impatient minutes, the attendants were able to calm him down. But that didn't last long, as the patient struggled with his captors once again.

Saber used his mouth, teeth and legs as weapons. It took all three male attendants to hold him down while the nurse injected him in his hip – right through his clothing and without pulling down his dirty pants – with three hundred milligrams of Thorazine, a depressant. A few minutes later, Saber was feeling the effects of the hypnotic drug. His rage finally began to subside, so the male attendants left the room. But the female nurse stayed behind while I questioned him – as he lay on the floor and stared at me.

Speaking loudly to keep his attention, I introduced myself. "Hello Mr. Saber. I'm Detective Zoolu. I would like to ask you a few questions about your wife's disappearance. Will you talk with me?"

As his eyes filled with tears, he blurted out, "Her head was cut off."

"What do you mean?" I asked him, looking into his crying eyes. "You saw someone cut off your wife's head?"

He didn't answer. He seemed to be in another world. I thought he had passed out because his eyes rolled back into his head. But a minute or so later, he opened his eyes. Then he began muttering to himself, but I couldn't understand what he was saying.

I continued with my questioning anyway. "Mr. Saber. How did your wife disappear?" I asked, loudly.

He answered me but I couldn't understand his gibberish because he was mumbling incoherently. But I could tell from his facial expression that he was trying to tell me about his wife's disappearance, but his words were incomprehensible. Then in a wink of an eye, he seemed like a completely different person, acting sane and normal…and began telling me his story.

"Somehow we arrived in this old, dirty, broken down town. A town that looked to be from the eighteen hundreds. Like an old western town you'd see in the movies," said a now soft-spoken Saber.

"Mr. Saber, how many people lived in the town?" I asked, knowing what the answer would be.

"Not many. In fact, I thought it was a ghost town until I saw one of the buildings with an "open" sign on its door."

"What kind of building?"

"It was a costume shop."

I continued my questioning. "What time of year was this?"

"If I remember correctly, it was a day or two before Halloween. Because we needed to rent costumes for a neighbor's Halloween party."

"Who told you about this costume shop?"

"Nobody. I don't know how we even got there. I keep asking myself that same question, day after day."

"Then why were you driving your car that day?"

He shrugged his shoulders. "We went out for a nice, quiet drive in the country. But an hour or so after we left the house, we ended up on this strange, mountain road."

"What was so strange about it?" I asked him, already knowing the answer.

"It came out of nowhere. One minute … No, strike that…one second we were driving on the main highway and the next second we were driving up a steep and winding, dirt road."

I asked him why he didn't turn his car around and go back the way he came.

"I'll tell you why. For one thing, the area looked foreign to me. I didn't have any idea where we were. There wasn't supposed to be any type of mountain around the area we were driving in. But yet, there it was."

"But you still haven't answered my question, Mr. Saber. Why didn't you turn your car around and head back the way you came?"

He told me he couldn't, adding, "Something had control of my body and my car. It was frightening."

I didn't want to talk about that phenomenon again so I changed the subject. "Let's get back to the costume shop. Why did you go in there?" I asked him.

He told me he wanted to ask for directions and find out where he was. "We looked on our map…the town wasn't on it. But when we entered the shop, we forgot about our troubles and began looking at the costumes."

"Did you like them?"

He nodded, adding, "They were immaculate, made of the finest materials, and you didn't have to leave a security deposit to rent them. So we picked out the costumes we liked and tried them on."

I asked him which ones they had chosen.

He told me they picked out costumes of the king and queen of England from the tenth century. "The costumes were exquisite. It was as if they were the actual clothes that the royal couple might have worn."

"Did you rent them?"

He nodded. "We decided to wear them back to our home. My wife was the first one out the front door and I followed right behind her," replied Saber, trying to hold back his tears, as he thought about his wife's death.

"Then what happened?" I asked, anxiously.

He too saw a giant flash of bright light. "As if an atom bomb had fallen right in front of us."

"So what did you do?"

"I stopped in my tracks, as if I was frozen in time. And just at that moment I saw a big man dressed in a black hood. I couldn't see his face, only his eyes, nose and mouth. He grabbed my wife and pushed her to her knees," said Saber, trying to catch his breath.

I could tell he was very tired and sleepy. So I told him, "If it's too much for you, we can wait a few more minutes to give you a chance to gather your strength?"

But he wouldn't hear of it. After a few loud and gruff coughs, he was ready to continue. "I'm okay now. As I was saying. When that hooded man pushed my wife to her knees, another man held her firmly by the shoulders and then the hooded man swung a giant axe and cut her head off. I saw it land in a basket, right in front of my feet."

I asked him why he didn't try and save his wife.

"I don't know," he replied, still lying on the floor. "I was frozen to the floor. I couldn't move my feet. Everything happened so fast I guess I was in shock."

I wanted to know more. "What happened after this hooded man cut off your wife's head?"

"Someone grabbed my wrists and tried to pull me out of the shop onto the wooden platform. But I was able to break free."

"So what happened next?"

"When I broke free, I fell backwards and hit my head on the door and was knocked out. The next thing I knew, I was in a hospital being treated for head injuries. After that, I was then driven to this place. I've been here ever since."

I asked him why the doctor hadn't released him, adding, "You sound rational to me."

"I am rational, damn it," he snapped. "But the doctors still refuse to release me. I haven't done anything wrong…and yet they keep me locked up in this lunatic asylum."

But I reminded him of his violent outburst when I first entered the room.

He replied, "If you crapped in your pants three times a day and had to wear a straightjacket twenty-four hours a day, you would be just a little angry too. Don't you think?"

"Mr. Saber, I guess I would. You do have a point."

"Please Mister," cried Saber. "If you have any pity in your heart, please help me get out of this place."

"I don't know what *I* could do."

But after looking into his sad eyes full of despair and hopelessness, I couldn't help but feel sorry for him. I decided then and there that I would do my best to find the truth behind all of these disappearances and put their stories to rest. Whether they were true or not.

"Well sir … You just hang in there," I told him. "I will do what I can. I promise you, I won't give up until I find the truth."

"Thank you, sir."

But before I departed I asked him one last question. "Mr. Saber … How old are you?" Hoping he was as old as he looked.

"I wondered when you were going to ask that question."

"Why?"

"Because I've been asked that question many times since I've been here."

"So, how old are you?"

He told me he was only thirty-three years old, adding, "I look twice that age, don't I?"

"Mr. Saber, I'm not going to lie to you, you do look older than thirty-three," I replied, not wanting to make him feel any worse than he was already. "What happened to you?"

He told me he started aging right after his visit to that evil, mysterious costume shop.

I just stared at him in silence. I was struck by the weird sensation that I too was growing older, faster than normal. That thought put a sour taste in my mouth. All of a sudden reality set in. Was this what I had to look forward to? But before I could dwell on the answer, the female nurse interrupted my deep train of thought.

"Detective, I think we should be going now," she said, pointing to a sleeping Saber.

"I guess so. He's no help to me now," I said as I watched Saber, asleep in his straightjacket on a dirty, cold and matted floor.

With that said the female nurse escorted me to the front door of the old building. But before walking to my car I thanked her for her help…and expressed interest in visiting again, sometime in the near future.

But now the day was nearly over. I had just enough time to return to the station, sign out, and return home for a goodnight's rest…and a stiff drink or two… or three?

CHAPTER 6

The next morning I arrived at work in a somewhat jovial mood. I decided to visit Jackson Billing again at his costume shop sometime today…to ask him a few more questions – like why some of his customers began aging at a rate ten times faster than normal. And why my detective friend, Detective Waters from Missing Persons, wasn't aging? His name was the one that my partner had written on the faded piece of paper. He supposedly, had driven out there. But if he had visited that shop, why wasn't he aging as rapidly as my witnesses had?

As I sat at my desk looking over my notes and investigative reports, I had many questions that needed answers: logical and bona fide answers. I decided to ask my friend in Missing Persons about his interview at the costume shop. Just as I left my desk, I noticed Detective Matthew from Paris Police Department enter through the front door. I walked over to him and shook his hand.

"How are you doing, Detective Matthew?" I asked.

He opened his mouth to speak but nothing came out. He just stared at my face, then after a few long seconds of silence, he said, "Man, what has happened to your face and hair? And you walk like you've thrown your back out of whack. Did you get into some kind of accident?"

I shrugged my shoulders and shook my head, no.

He added, "I just can't get over how much you've aged in the last week or so, since I saw you last." He then reached out with his hand and felt the wrinkles on my face.

"Please, don't remind me," I told him, knocking his hand away.

"What the heck happened to you?" Matthew asked, giving me a funny look.

I told him I didn't know. "But if I continue to age at this abnormal rate, I'm going to contact a good specialist. But enough talk about me. What brings you out this way?"

Matthew scratched his head, then replied, "I can't seem to find that damn town. I thought we could drive there together. If you have the time, that is?"

I assured him that I did.

He added, "I want to get a first-hand look at the place. And see if there is any validity to the weird stories that I have heard from the people I've interviewed?"

"Let's go," I told him.

"Do you want to take my car or yours?" he asked.

I told him that we'd take mine. "I've been there before, so I know the way. In fact, my car practically drives itself to that crazy town."

Detective Matthew thought I was kidding about my car driving itself, but I was dead serious.

"Good. I'm ready whenever you are," said Matthew.

I was anxious to leave…because I still had a few questions I wanted that funny, little man at that costume shop to answer.

And so did Matthew. He told me that he was investigating three different disappearances and there seemed to be a connection between his victims and that town.

I told him I was only concerned with one investigation – my partners. Adding, "The longer I investigate his case, more and more victims keep popping up. And all of them had visited that costume shop before they disappeared."

We walked out to the parking lot and hopped into my car. I had been there before, and knew what to expect. That's why I wanted to drive my car. I had Matthew follow the map as I drove so he would know which direction and which roads to use. Once he knew the way, he could drive out to the town without getting lost. Actually, he had no idea where it was. He only knew, after interviews with his witnesses, that the place was approximately a two-hour drive west of our city.

And to put it mildly, the town was fairly difficult to find. The roads weren't clearly marked and many times, weren't clearly seen. In fact, despite the many times that I had visited there, I'm still not sure about the directions? One second I'm driving on the main road and then, zap, I'm suddenly driving up a steep, mountain road – the car at times, driving itself.

The ride went well for the first hour and a half until I noticed that we were on the wrong road. I was sure of it because the surrounding landscape seemed foreign to me. And I didn't see any of the landmarks that I had seen before. To say the least, I was a little confused…and was undecided on a plan of action. So I remained silent, not mentioning my doubts to my passenger. But he didn't seem to notice that we were lost because he was too busy looking at the scenery.

So I continued driving in the same direction hoping I would soon see something I recognized. But two and a half-hours had passed. We should have been there by now, I thought to myself. Just at that moment, I think Matthew also knew we weren't going in the right direction.

"Matthew," I asked him, "take a look at that map that I drew. Are we going in the right direction?"

"I'm not sure?" he replied. "I thought you had been there before?"

"I have. I don't know what could have happened? I must have missed a turn? I'm sure we're driving in the right direction. We have to be. I can't believe this is happening," I said, pounding my fists on the steering wheel, venting my anger and frustration.

I pulled off to the side of the road to check the map. According to it, we were on the correct road. Either I didn't go far enough or I went too far. We decided to drive for another hour in the same direction before making a U-turn.

I was really confused and couldn't get over the fact that we had not come to the mountain road yet. I'd driven this way many times before and I knew we were driving in the right direction. But we should have run into that mountain road by now. Except it was nowhere in sight. I was, to say the least, very frustrated and mystified.

Finally, the hour had passed and we still hadn't reached the area, so I decided to turn around and head towards the station. Somehow I passed by that mountain road. But I was determined to find it.

"What are you doing?" asked Matthew.

"I'm going back the way we came. I missed the turn off to the mountain road. Before it only took me a little over two hours to get to that crazy town. I just don't understand what I did wrong."

"I sure don't know," exclaimed Matthew.

"You were looking at the map," I told him, "so you should have seen it? But we couldn't have missed that turn off. I'm sure of it."

Matthew tried to put me at ease, saying, "This happened to me when I tried to find the place almost two weeks ago. I don't know what I did wrong either. But I didn't have any map to use. I went on the directions of a few eyewitnesses."

"Believe me, Matthew, it's not that hard to find. I just drive on this main road for approximately two hours and this mountain appears out of nowhere. I don't understand why it isn't happening today."

Matthew was getting a little annoyed with my excuses. "You're the one that should know how to get there," he griped. "You've been there how many times?"

I shrugged my shoulders and said, "Maybe three or four times. One time when I went out there…the store was closed. But yeah, I've been out there at least three times if not more. I don't know what I did wrong today."

Matthew became angry and snarled, "Zoolu, I think you are doing this on purpose? You want to solve the case on your own."

"Why would I do that?"

Matthew replied, "Because you think I will take all your glory. But don't worry, I'm not interested in being the hero. I just want the disappearances to stop."

I reassured him and told him that I wasn't doing it on purpose. "You have the map…and should know if I'm going the right way or not?" Then I asked him if he wanted to drive?

He told me no. "This is your car…not mine. And yes, I have the map. But remember…it's your map. How do I know if it's correct or not?"

"I guess you'll have to take my word for it."

Matthew gave me a dirty look and said, "I guess I'll have to."

Trying to calm things down, I exclaimed, "We probably just missed the turn off. But we would have been able to see the mountain road if we had passed it."

My passenger remained silent…and seemed to be angry with me. Heck, I couldn't blame him. I was angry with myself.

We continued driving towards the station. An hour had passed since we had made the U-turn. We should have been on top of that mountain by now, I thought. I wondered if the evil spirits were keeping us away from that area. There was no other reasonable explanation. A mountain just doesn't disappear overnight. But yet, this one had.

Matthew broke the silence, saying, "We might as well drive back to your station. It's getting late and I have to drive all the way back to the state line, which takes me two hours to do. I'll just scratch this one up to experience."

"Listen," I told him. "This is the same way I went before when I drove to that town. When we get back to the station we'll go see the guy that has been there before and you can ask him if the map you are holding is correct or not."

"That's all right. I believe you. But I would like to know if this map is correct? I still haven't seen the turn that takes us to the mountain road. We must be on the wrong road."

"I'm telling you…this is the right road. It's not really a turn. This mountain, I swear, comes out of nowhere. We are on the right road. Something just doesn't want us to find the place today. I'm sure of it."

"If we're on the right road…then why haven't we found it yet?" Matthew asked, suspiciously.

"I honestly don't know. But Detective Waters might know why we couldn't find the area."

"Will he tell us if he knows?"

"Sure. Why not?" I answered. Adding, "I also want to ask him why he hasn't aged since visiting that costume shop and I have?"

Matthew gave me a quizzical and asked, "Do you really believe that? Is that what you think is happening to you?"

I nodded. "And I think it's happening to a few other people besides me."

Matthew was about to ask me about those other people.

But before he could utter another syllable, I nipped it in the bud. "Let's just leave it at that."

We drove all the way back to town without seeing any mountain road. At one point, we even pulled over to the side of the road, again, just to recheck the map. But it didn't help. It seemed the whole area just up and disappeared. That was the best way to explain it.

When we arrived back at the station, Detective Matthew was going to leave before we questioned Detective Waters. But I was able to talk him into staying for a few extra minutes.

After signing in at the front desk, we walked to Water's department to see if he was in. Luckily for us, he was. He was sitting at his desk drinking a cup of coffee and smoking a cigarette.

"Hello, Detective Waters. How are you doing today?" I asked, as Matthew and I walked up to his desk.

"Fine," he replied. "Have a seat. Now, what can I do for you?"

"Well, first, let me introduce you to my friend, Detective Matthew."

"I'm glad to meet you," said Waters.

After the two detectives shook hands, we took our seats and I explained to Waters the reason for the visit. "Detective Matthew works out of Missing Persons for the Paris State Police Department. He's investigating the disappearance of two people... similar to my investigation. But we ran into a problem today."

"Why, what happened?" Waters asked.

I explained to him that we had used the map that I had drawn and couldn't find the turn-off to the mountain road. I showed him the map.

"Where did you get that?" Waters asked, as he looked it over.

"I drew it for Matthews."

"That looks like the map I drew for Detective Webber."

"You drew one for him? I didn't find it," I told him. "I drew mine after I had already found the place."

"You just said you couldn't find it," Waters said

"I know, but I've been to that place at least three times. I remember when you told Webber about it. You told him...that he might not be able to find it...that some people can't find it at all. But you never said why."

Waters asked me if we drove for two hours on that main road.

I nodded and again told him that I'd been there before. "But today that mountain just wasn't there."

"Tell me...did you two travel in the same car?" he asked, smiling as if he knew the secret answer.

I nodded. "We drove in my car...just like I had done many times before."

"I know," Waters replied, "it's happened to me before, too. For some reason I've never been able to find that road, either...when I've had more than one male person in the car."

"Do you know why that is?" I asked.

He shook his head and told me he didn't have an answer. "But if you believe the legend...then there might be a possible explanation," he whispered, so others couldn't hear what he was talking about.

"Legend? What legend?" Matthew clamored.

The others in the room turned their attention towards him.

"Hush! Not so loud," cautioned Waters. "You want people to think you're wacko. We don't talk about that too much around here."

"Why not?" I asked him.

Waters gave me a funny look and said, "It tends to make one sound nutty and irrational. That's why I never went back to that crazy town."

Detective Matthew looked at me in utter confusion and acted as though Detective Waters and I were lying to him. So I had Matthews ask Detective Waters to verify if the map had been drawn correctly or not?

After looking at the map again, he replied, "Yep. That map is drawn correctly."

Matthew looked at me and then to Waters and said, "Well…if this map is right, then something's wrong with our eyesight, because we couldn't find that mountain. Why couldn't we find it?" Matthew looked at Waters for the answer.

Waters shrugged his shoulders and replied, "Next time…drive alone…and you shouldn't have any problem. Unless you can't read a map."

"I can read a map," Matthew snapped.

Looking at Matthew, Waters added, "I suggest you read up on the Legend of Hollow Pass."

"Why is that?" Matthew asked him, still seething after Waters' sarcastic remark.

"The gods might not want your soul."

"What are you talking about, Detective Waters?" Matthew asked, scratching his head.

But Detective Waters refused to answer him and hid his face in a newspaper.

"Are you ready to go, Detective Matthew?" I asked.

Matthew asked me why Waters wouldn't answer his question.

Just as I was about to give him my answer, Detective Waters clamored, "I told you, the gods might not want your soul."

With a startled and confused look on his face, Matthew griped, "Well I think I've heard enough. It's getting late and I still have a long drive ahead of me." Looking at me, he added, "I think the next time I want to visit that town, I'll take Waters' advice and follow behind you in my car."

"That's fine with me," I told him. "But knowing my luck, we'll just get lost again."

Detective Matthew said goodbye and walked away, while I stayed behind to ask Waters a few more questions.

"Detective Waters, do you really believe all that crap you just spewed out of your mouth?" I asked.

"Of course I do," he answered. "Why? Don't you?"

After a few long seconds of silence, I changed the subject. I asked him if he noticed anything different about my appearance than when he saw me last?

After a long pause, he looked into my eyes and replied, "Well I didn't want to say anything about it...but you better slow down with your partying. You're getting old, fast."

Pointing to the wrinkles on my face, I retorted, "So you did notice. But it's not from partying. It seems everyone I've interviewed that has visited that costume shop ages much faster than normal."

But Waters acted as though he didn't know anything about it. "Is that right?" he replied, rubbing his chin. "I don't think I've gotten any older...at least not since the last time I looked in the mirror."

"That's what I can't understand. You haven't gotten any older...but yet all the other people that I've talked to that <u>have</u> entered that costume shop...have all aged at an accelerated rate."

Waters then told me something that surprised me – that he never went inside the shop. "I always stayed outside of it. All my interviews were done outside...on the porch."

"Are you telling me that you interviewed that hunchback, old man outside?"

He shook his head, no. He explained to me that the old man was inside the shop while he was standing outside on the porch.

"Then you don't believe in all that stuff about evil spirits and curses?"

He gave me a quizzical look and replied, "I never believed the stories that the witnesses told me…if that's what you're referring to."

"Then what do you think happened to your victims?"

He leaned forward on his desk and looking me in the eyes, he answered, "I believed then…and I believe now, that their spouses ended up leaving with another partner and started a new life in another state."

For some reason I didn't believe him. I had a gut feeling that something was askew and asked him about it. "If you don't believe their stories, then how do you account for all the mysterious things happening in that area?"

"Such as?"

"Like what happened to us today. We couldn't find the place even though we had the map right in front of us…and I know we were on the right road."

But Waters challenged my explanation and told me that I must have been on the wrong road. "You made an honest mistake."

But I didn't. And told him so. "Remember…this is the same road that I had driven on three or four times before. And each time…had taken me right to that crazy town."

"Then what can I tell you. I'm sure you'll figure it out eventually."

"When?" I asked.

"When you think you have had enough, you'll know what to do."

"I bet you finished your investigation as fast as it started! Once you interviewed your witnesses…you probably figured they were quacks or nut cases and closed your investigation. I'm right, aren't I?"

"So what?" snapped Waters. "You do your job and I'll do mine. To close an investigation you have to have a good reason. My reasoning was very sound and logical. Plus, there wasn't any evidence to the contrary to disprove my theory."

"What about the eyewitness reports from the spouse or partner of the missing people?" I asked him.

"Their stories were irrelevant. I listened to them and put their opinions to the side."

"You ought to be proud of yourself, Waters, for doing such thorough investigations. I'd like you to tell your side of it to the two people I interviewed at the nuthouse."

"Why should I?" he snarled.

I leaned forward getting as close to him as I could and replied, "Because they also came across that little, hunchback and his costume shop. And ended up living at the mental institution for telling the truth. I hope you can sleep at night."

"I sleep fine," Waters replied, smiling. "I have nothing to be ashamed of."

"Well, when I find out what really happened to those people…then we'll see if we can't reopen your missing person investigation that you closed prematurely. Then we'll see how good you sleep at night," I said as I arose from my chair then stormed out of the room.

I was very frustrated. I still didn't have any concrete evidence to show that the little, old man was the evil culprit. I did find out, however, one answer to the question of my rapid aging. After listening to Detective Waters, I now believed you had to have gone inside the shop to be exposed to the rapid aging disease. I was sure of that. Now I had to find out how to reverse this crazy and mysterious disease.

That and many other crazy questions swished around inside my head until I looked at my watch and saw that it was past quitting time.

I had worked all day long and hadn't had a bite to eat. I was absolutely famished. I wanted to stop at Gabriele's and buy one or two of my favorite steak and cheese hoagies. But I wanted a drink even more. So I drove straight past the cafe and continued towards home.

COSTUME SHOP

The first thing I did when I arrived home was to walk directly to the kitchen. I didn't have the time to buy a small liquor cabinet for the living room, yet, so I still had to walk to the kitchen cabinet to get my bottle of liquid dreams. After grabbing a full bottle of scotch, I strolled into the living room and plopped myself down on my comfortable couch before pouring shot after shot and drinking them just as fast.

I just needed to relax and forget about work. But it was never easy. I kept thinking about tomorrow's course of action that would improve my investigations.

I decided I wanted to visit that crazy town the following day. I was going to find that place even if it took me twenty hours of driving to get there. And as an added attraction I would bring along my bottle of scotch. So I could test my theory that alcohol would block the spirit or evil entity before it could take control of my mind and body. I also wanted to check my photocopies against the photos on the costume shop wall to see if the town looked now, like it did back in the eighteen sixties. And to compare the old man with the old man in that picture – to see if they were one and the same. Or if it was just one of his long, lost relatives?

And I also wanted to question that old Indian man again and that strange boy, that is, if I could find him.

These thoughts continued to swirl through my head. And the more I thought about my investigation, the more I drank. And the more scotch I drank, the cloudier my mind became, until I finally drifted off to sleep. But my dream turned into a nightmare – about that little hunchback and his costume shop. I found myself inside the shop teasing him, trying to get him to come out from behind his little counter. But he never moved from that spot and stayed perched in his little cubicle all day long. I aggravated him to the point of no return.

I began by throwing costumes from shelf to shelf. Or taking parts of one costume and trading it with another. I could see this was getting to him. In fact, he became so angry that his face turned a beet red and steam rose from his balding head and deformed shoulders.

I continued messing up the costumes until the old man couldn't stand it a minute longer. Jumping from behind his little cubicle, he finally came after me. When he did this, he startled me. But now I knew why he stayed behind the counter – he wasn't completely human. He was half man and half beast. His lower half was that of a goat. He had long, dirty, brown hair from his waist all the way down his two legs and two hooves, and sticking out from his behind was a long, hairy tail that had a sharp, forked point on the end of it. He walked upright like a human, but very unbalanced. And his hooves made a loud clopping sound that reverberated inside the shop. I couldn't believe what I was seeing. It looked too real to be a costume.

When he jumped out from behind his cubicle, he stomped his right hoof five or six times, snorted, then took a very deep breath and began inhaling my whole body into his own. That's when I awakened from my deep sleep, my body sopped in sweat.

Looking at my alarm clock I saw that it was nearly time for work and decided to get out of bed. But I had a terrible hangover to shake. After lighting a cigarette I walked into the kitchen and waited for my automatic coffee maker to respond, which produced hot, black coffee within thirty seconds. For the next two hours, I drank coffee, cleaned up and got ready for work. By the time I got behind the wheel of my car, my hangover had nearly disappeared, although I was still a little drunk. But not enough to forget my bottle of scotch –which I would use to try out my theory when I visited that mysterious area later that day.

CHAPTER 7

When I arrived at the station I quickly signed in at the front desk then headed for the snack room for a cup of black coffee and a jelly-filled donut. I hadn't had anything in my stomach for almost a day and a half. This investigation was eating me alive. I was adamant about finding a plausible explanation to the weird happenings in that desert area.

As I was walking to my desk, Captain Bird stopped me and invited me into his office. He was already sitting behind his desk when I entered the room.

"Take a seat, Detective," said Captain Bird.

"Good morning, Captain Bird."

"I called you in here to see how your investigation of Detective Webber's disappearance was going? Have you learned of his whereabouts, yet?"

"Not yet. But I'm working on a few different angles. I don't want to say much more than that, for now," I said, as I chewed on one of my fingernails.

"Are you feeling all right, Detective? You haven't been looking like your old self lately. You look as though you've aged ten years since you started your investigation."

"I'm fine. I must have caught the flu," I lied.

"I'm wondering now if I did the right thing by letting you investigate your partner's disappearance, instead of giving it to Missing Person's?"

"So what answer did you come up with?"

"I didn't. But I asked Detective Waters about it."

"What did he have to say?"

"After speaking with him, he insisted you take the case. So, against my better judgment, I listened to good detectives instead of my own intuition. But I'm worried about you," exclaimed Captain Bird.

"Don't be."

"You look like hell. When this investigation is completed, I want you to take a vacation for a couple of weeks. You look as though you could use one."

"Thanks, Captain. I guess I have been working a little too hard on this investigation. But he was my partner. I am going to find out his whereabouts or die trying," I said, pounding my fists on his desktop.

"Well, I wouldn't go that far. Just don't overdo it. I've already lost one detective in your department. I don't want to lose another. Get me?"

"I understand, Captain. In fact, I'm going out to that area where Detective Webber was last seen, later today."

"When?"

"I'm going to be leaving in about an hour."

"Do you have any suspects or any eyewitnesses?"

"I'm working on it, Captain. I've interviewed a few eyewitnesses, but nothing solid, yet. I still have more investigative work to do. But I promise you, I will come up with the answer to my partner's disappearance."

"Is there anyone that you have your eye on?" he asked, as he lit a cigarette and blew out a big, cloud of smoke that made me cough.

"I've got my sights set on a prime suspect. In fact, I'm going to interview him sometime today," I replied, coughing in between my words, but nonetheless, sounding very confident.

"Good. I'll let you get back to work. I've wasted enough of your time. Now get out of my office!"

I walked back to my desk as all the eyes in the room were staring at me as I sat down in my chair. I didn't know what they were looking at or why. I just ignored their stares. I knew my body was changing right in front of their eyes. But what could I do about it? I kept to myself and didn't say much to anyone, especially about my investigation. I was sure they wouldn't understand my situation or my explanation. So why try?

I sat in the chair reading over my notes that I had taken during the interview with my two eyewitnesses from the nuthouse.

Once I had gotten my thoughts in order, I was ready for another mysterious ride. I just hoped I could find the place. Too many strange things were happening in that area. Whether it was spirits or some weird force that had taken control of my mind and body, I didn't know?

But I was certainly going to try out my drinking theory. Will the strange force overtake my being, even when I am completely drunk or will it just get the spirits drunk too? That is, if they were really the ones that were stealing my mind and body? If that's the case, then maybe I could control the spirits and find out why they were doing this?

I signed out at the front desk and headed for that crazy, dilapidated town. The minute I turned on to the main highway, I started trying out my theory. I began drinking, swig after swig of my twenty-year-old scotch. I wanted to be good and drunk by the time I reached that mountain road. I knew I shouldn't take the chance of driving while drinking, but there never was any other traffic on the road and I usually had complete control and quick reaction time, even while I was drunk. So if my plan worked I was pretty confident that I would be in complete control of all my faculties. I was certain I could drive with the utmost of caution. So I continued to drink and drive.

Almost two hours later, I was driving up that narrow, winding, mountain road. Once again, it seemed to come out of nowhere. When I looked into my rear-view mirror, I couldn't see the main road behind me. I knew I *had* to be on the main road. But that just couldn't be. I was driving the exact same way the day before with Detective Matthew but for some reason couldn't find this mountain road. Now I had.

My bottle of scotch was now completely empty and I still had control of my driving, but barely. Luckily, I didn't see any other vehicles on the road during my two-hour drive.

Within five minutes of finishing the bottle, I was feeling pretty drunk. My head began to spin and suddenly it became very hard to keep control of the vehicle. And just at that moment, the weather turned violent. A hard rain pummeled my car, while the clouds and mist smothered it.

As I reached the peak of the mountain the car suddenly veered to the right, down a deep slope. The violent winds began to shake and pound the car so violently that I thought it would shake the car apart. Moments later, giant balls of hail bounced off the body of the car. The wind picked the car up and tossed it from one side of the road to the other. The foggy mist became so thick there was zero visibility.

Then suddenly I felt something grow over and through my whole body. I couldn't move a muscle. My hands gripped the steering wheel so tightly that I bent it. I couldn't move my head at all. I could only look straight ahead into the windshield. My theory didn't work. All it did was make me drunk, dizzy and sleepy. This evil spirit or entity took control of my mind and body even when I was stone drunk.

Again the wind and hail had left its mark on my car.

When the car had finally reached the bottom of the canyon, I again had regained control of my being. I could think, once again. I wasn't quite as sharp as usual because I was as drunk as a mouse on catnip.

The weather had calmed to a gentle breeze and the foggy mist had dissipated completely.

My eyes focused on the road in front of me. Ahead of me, I thought I saw that old, Indian man, Wallahoo Cecil, walking on the side of the road, heading towards the town. I was still a few hundred feet away from the hulking figure, but for some strange reason I couldn't catch up to him. I was driving forty to forty-five miles an hour and that huge Indian stayed the same distance ahead of me.

I thought I would never catch up to that old Indian man, but I did...or at least I thought I did. By the time I was about to pull alongside of him, his hulking figure just disappeared right in front of my drunken eyes. I could have sworn it was Wallahoo Cecil carrying something under his arm, possibly a costume to sell to the hunchbacked, old man? But I must have been hallucinating from the excessive amount of alcohol I had ingested.

When I arrived at the costume shop I pulled up next to another car. So I figured the shop had visitors.

As I stepped out of the car I could barely walk. I more or less stumbled my way to the shop. When I had finally reached the front door I had to stop and catch my breath. My vision was still very blurry and my head was still spinning, but I had the strength to push my drunken body forward into the shop.

When I entered, I noticed the old man, Jackson Billing, behind the counter talking with that old Indian man, Wallahoo Cecil. I watched as he handed the hunchbacked, old man a cloth bundle. But as I focused my eyes to the darkness of the shop, the old, Indian man suddenly disappeared in a puff of smoke. He was gone…again. After rubbing my eyes and scratching my head, I just figured it was either my eyes or my drunken stupor playing tricks on me.

While in my drunken stupor I also noticed two young adults roaming around the shop, a man and a woman. They were searching through the racks of costumes.

I slowly walked up to the counter and tried to focus my eyes on the wall photo behind the counter. The first couple of seconds I stared at it the photo remained clear. But suddenly, the picture blurred before my eyes. But what I did see was that the picture on his wall and the photo I had photocopied from the library looked exactly alike. Although the photo and picture were clear, the details and faces were too small and blurry to positively tell one hundred percent if the two men in the photos were the same person.

The little, hunchbacked, old man didn't say a word to me. He was brushing off the dirt from one of his costumes. It looked like the same bundle of clothes that mysterious Indian had given to him. But it couldn't be, I thought to myself. The Indian had been just a figment of my imagination or an illusion.

But this young couple sure wasn't. They were making quite a mess in that little shop. They had tried on costume after costume and had left them scattered all around the shop. When Mr. Billing yelled at them for making such a mess and not cleaning up after themselves, the young couple became even more outrageously disrespectful to the old man and his shop. They began throwing the beautiful and exquisite costumes on the floor and then stepped on them with their dirty shoes. The young male even snorted snot onto one of the exquisite, one-of-a-kind costumes. Suddenly, I saw that old man's face turn a fire engine red. He was livid.

The two, outlandish customers continued to laugh and party at the expense of the hunchback. He was becoming very angry and upset at the disrespectful actions of this young couple. Steam began rising from his head, just like in my nightmare. But this was actually happening. His eyes were bulging out of their sockets. I thought the little old man might explode with anger and throw those kids out on their rear ends. But he surprised me. He remained cool-headed and just ignored their ridiculous actions. But I couldn't. I yelled at them to be quiet and to respect the rules of the store. But they just ignored me.

The young couple continued to walk to and from the changing room, changing into one costume after another. I had counted at least a dozen different changes of costumes that they each had tried on. They continued to be rowdy, disruptive and disrespectful. I stared at them in disbelief. Then the man strode over to me and got right into my face. I thought he was going to hit me with his fists. But instead, he yelled at me.

"Mind your own business, Mister," snarled the young man. "I'll do whatever I want. Nobody tells me what to do. Understand?"

Then he just nonchalantly walked over to his girlfriend and continued to pick through the costumes.

Finally, the little, hunchback spoke up. "Listen, you kids. Why don't you try on the gangster costumes? If you want to act like thugs, why don't you dress the part? There are two costumes to the left of where you are standing."

"What costumes are you talking about?" asked the young man, holding up his arms in frustration.

"It's the Bonnie and Clyde costumes. They even come with their own Tommy guns. I'll let you rent them at cost and you won't have to leave a security deposit," said Jackson Billing, as I watched and listened.

The guy thought about the idea for a minute then looked at his girlfriend. Their eyes lit up, a smile broke upon both their faces and then they nodded in agreement.

"Yep, that sounds like an excellent choice. Sweetheart, let's try these on," said the young man, as he handed his girlfriend the Bonnie and Clyde costumes, and walked to the small, changing room.

There was barely enough room for one person to change clothes in that little area in the back room. But, they both entered the room together. How they did it was beyond belief. But they somehow managed to undress and change into their costumes.

Within ten minutes, the two young adults were showing off their new wardrobe. Their bodies fit the costumes, perfectly, as if the costumes were tailor made just for them. The young couple seemed to portray the two gangsters exceptionally well. They were the spitting image of the real Bonnie and Clyde. They each carried their Tommy guns as though they had used them many times before. When they walked up to the counter and faced the little hunchbacked old man, I thought they were going to rob the place. In fact, I thought the young man was reaching for a gun in his waistband, but he was actually going for his wallet.

"What do we owe you for the costume rental?" asked the young man, as he began play acting and pointing the Tommy gun at the body of Jackson Billing as he sat behind the counter.

"It's ten dollars per costume. They must be returned in the same condition as they were issued. If they are damaged, it is up to the customer to pay for the repairs," said Billing, pointing to the sign on the wall behind him and the rules of his store.

"Here you go," said the young man, as he handed the old man twenty dollars.

"No. You pay me when you return the costumes. The only other rule in the rental agreement is that you must wear the costumes out of the shop."

"Why is that?" asked the female.

"Because once the costume has left the shop, you can't exchange it."

"We wouldn't do that. We like these costumes. They fit us perfectly," said the young man, as his girlfriend nodded in agreement.

"Yes, but sometimes a person can go to two or three parties during the three day rental agreement."

"So what?" snapped the young man.

"Please, let me finish my statement."

"So, go ahead. Speak."

"Thank you. As I was saying, they would wear one costume to one party and then return it for a different costume to wear at a following party. So, we refuse the return of the costume once it is rented."

"That doesn't make any sense. Why do that?"

"We feel that once you wear it, you won't want to return it. That is our store policy."

"That's fine with us. In fact, we will leave our regular clothes here and pick them up when we return the costumes," said the young man, as he handed two bundles of clothes to the old man.

"That's not store policy, but I guess it's all right if you leave them with me. I'll put them here behind the counter."

The young man and woman walked away with one arm wrapped around each other's waist and carried their Tommy guns in the other. Just as they reached the front door of the shop, I turned to look at the photos on the wall again. I was mystified by the close resemblance of the shop owner and the person in the photo.

While staring at the photo, I felt a warm breeze, as the young couple opened the front door to leave the shop. Then, out of the corner of my eye, I saw a bright, flash of light, possibly a flash of lightning but I couldn't tell. It was overwhelming. At that same instant, I heard what I thought was gunfire. I turned to look towards the open door and was shocked and amazed at what I saw.

Not only did I hear gunfire, but also I saw the young couple that had just left the shop, sitting in a model 'T' automobile. They were being shot at by a dozen or so law enforcement officers. The police must have fired hundreds of rounds of ammunition at the two, young gangsters. Some of the bullets were hitting and ricocheting off of the front of the dilapidated, wooden shop. So, I rushed to the front door and slammed it shut. I threw myself to the floor of the shop, so I wouldn't get hit by one of the flying bullets. Even though I was drunk, I still had very quick reflexes. While lying there, I wondered if I wasn't imagining or hallucinating all of this insanity, as I had the old Indian.

Once the door was shut, the gunfire seemed to stop almost instantly. I staggered to my feet, and opened the front door to look at the death and destruction of that young couple. But there was nothing to see. There was no car, no couple, no law enforcement people, nothing. All was quiet, just as it had been when I had first arrived in the town. The street was clean. There wasn't any sign of the young man and woman that had walked out of the shop as Bonnie and Clyde. Or their car.

I turned and looked at the little, hunchbacked, old man and the bulging eyes peering through his thick-lensed glasses as he smiled in victory. It was as though he knew what was going to happen. He had a sly look on his face, as though he had rid himself of two big problems. I just had to open the door again to see if I had imagined all of this insanity.

I looked all around the town. Nothing was out of order. I remembered hearing the bullets hitting the front of the shop, so I turned to look for any bullet holes in the old, wooden building. Sure enough, I saw what I believed to be three or four different bullet holes. I searched in my pants pocket for my penknife so I could dig out one of the bullets from the wall of the building. I picked at the first hole near the bottom of the door. Searching the hole for only a few seconds, I found my first lead bullet.

Searching the other holes, I found two more lead bullets. I couldn't prove that they had come from the gunfire that I had just heard, but they helped me believe what I thought I had seen. It also proved I hadn't been hallucinating. I placed the three bullets into a small, plastic evidence bag and placed it into my jacket pocket for safekeeping.

I walked down the stairs and out into the street to check for any other evidence that might prove my own eyewitness' testimony. I still needed some hard, indisputable evidence before I could tell my story to anyone. The three bullets that I had just uncovered were a start, but could easily be refuted without some other substantial evidence to back up my theory that this place did exist. I couldn't find anything to back up my claim, (other than those bullets) that two people dressed up as Bonnie and Clyde had their bodies ripped apart by hundreds of rounds of ammunition that had been fired by several law enforcement officers. This is what I thought I had seen in my drunken stupor.

I searched the surrounding area for over an hour before I had returned to the shop to confront the hunchbacked, old man. I wanted to get his reaction to what had just transpired. Now I was an eyewitness to the disappearance of the young couple dressed up as Bonnie and Clyde. And I wanted to make sure I wasn't going to end up at a mental institution like the last couple of eyewitnesses.

Before I entered the shop, I took three deep breaths to gather my courage then entered the shop and faced the shop owner. He seemed to be waiting for my questions.

"Well, Mr. Billing. I'm sure you saw what happened to that young couple that left your shop dressed as Bonnie and Clyde. Didn't you?"

"What? What happened to that couple?" he asked, peering over his glasses, smiling, as if he had just heard a good joke. "They left the shop like two, happy, young lovers. I'm not aware of anything else happening to them. Are you?"

"You know what happened to those kids and I think you wanted it to happen?" I snarled, getting very close to his face as I leaned across the counter. "That's why you suggested they wear the Bonnie and Clyde costumes. You knew they would be shot to death."

"Is that what you really think happened? That they were murdered just like the real Bonnie and Clyde had been cut down? That sounds mighty far-fetched to me."

"I don't care how fishy it sounds. That's what I saw take place."

"Come now, Detective. You do have quite the imagination. Don't you?"

"Mr. Billing, you honestly believe that nothing happened to that young couple? If it wasn't gunfire that I heard, then what are these?" I asked, as I held the clear, plastic, evidence bag that contained the three bullets in his face.

"What is that? Just some old bullets from some hunter's gun. That's not proof of anything."

"I know what I saw."

"You're drunk. Look at you. You can barely stand up," snapped Jackson Billing, as I leaned against the counter to balance myself.

"I still know what I saw. Nothing will ever change that. Nothing will change what the other eyewitnesses saw, either."

"If they saw what you just described, they must be crazy like you, too."

"They are honest and decent citizens."

"Oh, yes. The two individuals that you interviewed at the nuthouse. Those are some reliable witnesses."

"What about the similarities between you and the man in my photo taken more than one hundred and thirty years ago during the Civil War days?" I asked, placing my photo on the counter in front of him to look at.

"As far as me looking like the guy in your photo, what can I say? My family has been in this area for near two hundred years," Billing replied, as an evil smile appeared on his cherub round face. "Believe what you want."

I pounded my fist on the glass countertop. "You think you have outsmarted me. But you haven't. I'm still aware of the situation that transpired, here. So, when I get some corroborative evidence to back up my story, I'll come back here with a search warrant and tear this shack down."

"Do what you think needs to be done?"

"Oh, believe me, I will," I promised him. "Then I'll search the surrounding area for any bodies that you might have buried out there in the desert. I'll be all over you, like flies on dog crap. You won't have a minute of peace. I'll make certain of that."

"You have no proof that I've done anything illegal," Billing replied angrily. "You can accuse me all you want, but you won't do it here. Now get out of my shop!"

I hesitated to leave. But after his prodding, I stumbled out of the costume shop and into my car. I slowly drove away from that mysterious and crazy town. Maybe, the old, hunchbacked, Mr. Billing was right and I was just too drunk to realize that what I had seen had been hallucinations and nothing more? My crazy thoughts were exploding throughout my brain. How was I going to get anybody to believe my strange story, without sounding like an utter fool or nut case?

A few minutes after leaving that shop, I was heading back towards that mountain road. A few hundred yards ahead, I thought I saw that huge, hulking, male figure, again. This time walking away from the town, the same way as I was driving. I pushed the accelerator to the floor, so I could catch up to that very large figure. I hoped it was that old, Indian man, Wallahoo Cecil. I wanted to ask him a few more questions concerning

Jackson Billing and his costume shop. I seemed to get closer to him, but I could never catch up to him, for some unknown reason. I still didn't know for certain, if it was that Indian or not?

Approximately twenty feet away from the hulking figure, I ran into bad weather. I had just started climbing the mountain road and my body and mind began feeling the force of that invisible entity. Once again, it took over my being and my vehicle. The force was too strong to fight. My drunken stupor, again, had no effect on this spirit.

The rain, hail and fog seemed to pounce on my vehicle all at once. I tried to turn my head towards the side of the road to look for the old, Indian man, but I couldn't do it. The mysterious, invisible entity wouldn't allow it. Wallahoo Cecil should have been a few feet ahead of my vehicle, but he had suddenly disappeared. I was certain I hadn't passed him up. Even though the fog was very thick, I still had about ten feet of visibility. As my car neared the mountain peak, the weather became much fiercer. The hail once again, pounded large dents into the body of my car and the wind continued to toss the car around as if it was a small pebble.

Suddenly, a large gust of wind picked up the car and threw it high and far into the air. I had absolutely no control. The car, finally, landed quite a long distance from where it had been picked up. It came crashing down onto the road and veered towards the edge of the cliff. I tried to close my eyes, fearing the worst, but suddenly something grabbed hold of the car and positioned it back on the road.

Within a few minutes, I had reached the top of the mountain still in one piece. As the foul weather raged on, the car began accelerating on its own, descending quite rapidly as I headed towards the station. The spirit still had control of my being and car. Whatever it was, the entity had overpowered me. Even while I was drunk, I couldn't fight it.

As the car rumbled down the mountain road towards my town, the wind began to pick up, again. In fact, it picked my vehicle up again and threw it farther down the mountain. The car crashed to the dirt road with a hard thud and began to weave back and forth across the narrow, winding mountain road. I tried, with all my might to regain control of the car with no avail. But a split second later, I felt that spirit leave my body. I held on to the steering wheel and brought the car to a halt. I looked around to catch my breath and saw a clear sky above me. The foul, evil weather had disappeared and the sun appeared in the distance. Suddenly, out of nowhere, I was sitting in my car on the side of the main highway. Just as quickly as it had returned, the mountain road and mountain had disappeared.

Just as I pulled onto the highway, I suddenly saw two shining and flashing, red lights in my rear-view mirror. I was very shocked to say the least because I was being pulled over by a police car.

CHAPTER 8

Where did this police car come from, I thought to myself? I pulled over to the side of the road and sat shaking as I waited for the police officer to walk up to my window. I just hoped and prayed that he wouldn't notice that I was stone drunk. I tried to act sober, but it was useless. If I had been Paul Newman, I still couldn't have acted my way out of this situation. I was still trying to figure out what I was going to say to the officer as he walked towards my vehicle. My mouth was dry and my Adams apple stuck in my throat. The officer strolled up to my window, then bent forward to ask me a question.

"You were driving pretty erratic back there, weren't you sir?" asked the officer, as he peered into my vehicle, spotting my empty scotch bottle.

"It wasn't my fault, officer. My brakes went out coming down that steep mountain road," I said, trying to talk myself out of a traffic citation or worse yet, jail.

"Excuse me. But what mountain are you talking about?" asked the officer, looking over his shoulder for the mountain.

"The mountain that's right behind us," I replied, pointing my finger in that direction.

"Would you please step out of your vehicle, sir?"

I pleaded with him as I stumbled out of the vehicle. "Please, I have a logical explanation."

"Turn around and place your hands on top of your car."

"Please," I begged, as the police officer searched my person. "I'm a detective. I'm on an investigation."

"Take out your wallet and driver's license," barked the officer, as I turned to face him to hand him my license. "You smell of alcohol. Have you been drinking, today?" he asked, leaning close to my face and smelling my breath.

At first I didn't answer. I refused to answer. But the more I thought about it, I decided to tell him why I had been drinking.

"I know you won't believe me," I said, slurring my words. "But I'm investigating my partner's disappearance. I drove out to the town where he was last seen."

"And what town is this, you're talking about, sir?" asked the officer, as he looked at my driver's license and identification.

"It's a very weird and mysterious town. Every time I drive through that area, many strange things happen to me." I didn't want to say anything more 'cause it might get me into more trouble.

"What kind of strange things?" he asked me.

I hesitated for a few seconds not wanting to sound too crazy but figured I had no other choice but to tell the truth.

"When I start driving up that mountain, the weather gets real nasty. Then something takes control of my body and mind. It also controls the car," I said, hoping he'd believe me.

"I think I asked you this before? What mountain?" asked the officer, turning his head in every direction, looking for my mysterious mountain. "There aren't any mountains around this area. Not that I know of, anyway."

"It's right behind us. It's only one or two hundred yards down the road."

"I'm sorry, sir," said the officer, still eyeing my police identification. "I think you're mistaken or you're thinking about another road somewhere else."

"Believe me, Officer," I said, wobbling to and fro, as I leaned against my car to steady myself. "I know what I've told you sounds crazy but it's the truth."

"Mr. Zoolu, I see from your driver's license and your police identification that you are a homicide detective. But you said you are investigating a disappearance, not a homicide. Is that true?"

"Yes, that's true."

"I never heard of a police force like that. They use a Missing Person's detective to investigate murders and they use homicide detectives for missing person's investigations. That sounds normal to me. Now, what town did you say you just came from?"

I knew the officer was being sarcastic but I continued on with my story anyway.

"You know, I don't think I ever knew the name of it. I have a photo of it in my pants pocket." I dug deep into my pocket and pulled out the photo. "Here it is," I said, as I handed it to him.

"Are you serious? This town was burned down back in the late eighteen hundreds. I think you're just a little too inebriated."

"What are you talking about? I was at that town just a little while ago. In fact, I dug these out of one of the wooden buildings," I said, as I showed the officer the bag of bullets and watched as he inspected them.

"You want me to believe that you just dug these out of a building that was burned down over a hundred and thirty years ago?" asked the officer, holding out the bag of bullets.

"Yes, I do, Officer. In fact, I got them out of the wall of this building." I pointed to the building in the photo. "And I believe I talked with this man," pointing to the same photo. "You wouldn't believe what I've seen and experienced since I started investigating my partner's disappearance."

"Why don't you tell me? I know you want to," said the officer, crossing his arms in front of his chest, waiting to hear my next outrageous claim.

"I actually saw a young couple disappear right before my eyes."

"I think you've said enough. You are talking like an irrational person."

"I know it sounds crazy, but it's true."

"If you continue with your outrageous claims, you may be looking for another job."

"I knew I shouldn't have opened up my big mouth," I said, accidentally spitting on the officer as I spoke.

"I don't think I would tell your story to anyone else," said the officer, wiping my sloppy spit from his shirt and face. "They may not excuse your drunken behavior."

"I'm sorry about that," I said, as I tried to help the officer wipe the spit from his clothes.

"The only reason I'm giving you a break is due to the fact that you're a fellow law enforcement officer. But I'm still going to have to call it in. I'm still going to have to notify your superiors or your Captain."

The police officer placed me into the back seat of his patrol car while he called his superiors and mine about this situation? I was getting angry at him for not allowing me to drive home and for notifying my superiors. I pleaded with the young officer to free me, but he wouldn't listen. He didn't hear a word I was saying, as I begged and pleaded to be released. He ended up driving me back to my station.

Captain Bird met us at the front door as the young officer handed me over. Without saying a word to Captain Bird, or me, the young officer walked back to his patrol car and left the station's parking lot.

As I entered the front door to the station, I could feel my Captain's anger pierce through my old, drunken body.

"Come with me, Detective Zoolu," snapped Captain Bird, as I slowly staggered towards him and followed him to his office. "Take a seat, before you fall down." He pointed to the chair directly in front of his desk.

"I'm sorry for all the confusion, Captain," I said, as I bowed my head in shame and sat in the chair.

"Confusion. That's the least of my problems. What's all this nonsense you told the police officer about some town you had supposedly visited that had burned down over one hundred and thirty years ago? What are you trying to do to our police department? Make it the laughing stock of the country?"

"No, sir. I'm just trying to do my job."

"Your job!" barked Captain Bird, as he waved his arms about, like a band leader, leading his musicians. "If any of this gets out, which I'm sure it will, we both may be looking for new jobs."

"I'm sorry, sir. I didn't know it would go this far," I said, trying to apologize for my drunken behavior.

"You're not the type of officer to be drinking on the job. When did you start that?"

"I drank to try out a theory of mine. But it didn't work."

"Which theory is that?"

"If I tell you, you are not going to believe me."

"Try me," said Captain Bird, leaning back in his chair, waiting to hear my story.

"Captain, I had told you before that I was visiting the last place my partner was seen before he had disappeared. It was that town that had burned down."

"A town that no longer exists."

"Every time, I have visited that place, strange things seem to happen to me. Something seems to take over my mind and body."

"Yeah, alcohol."

"Captain, I thought, by getting blind drunk that spirit or entity, or whatever it was that had been taking control of my person, wouldn't be able to control me."

"Listen to yourself. Do you know how that sounds to a rational person?"

"Yes I do, Captain. But my idea didn't work anyway. I still didn't have any control of my being or my car for that matter. In fact, the police officer that drove me to the station today told me the town doesn't exist, just like you're saying."

"It doesn't. It burned down nearly one hundred and thirty years ago, Zoolu. Your story just doesn't sound rational."

"Captain, I'm being chastised for telling the truth. I believe that the owner of the costume shop, a hunchbacked, old man by the name of Jackson Billing, had something to do with my partner's disappearance."

"Have you interviewed this man, yet?"

"Yes, I have, sir."

"Have you run his name through our computer files or the FBI criminal data bank for a background check to find out just who this man is?"

"I think he is the same man in the photo that I have here in my pocket." I then handed Captain Bird the photo of the town and the townspeople that I had photocopied at the library.

"This is the town that you visited?" asked my Captain, as he pointed to the picture.

"Yes, that is the town and that is the man that owns the costume shop," I said, pointing to the man in the photo.

"Detective Zoolu, this picture was taken during the Civil War. That man would be more than one hundred and thirty years old by now. It even states under the picture that the town burned down in the late eighteen sixties."

"Yes, I know that, sir."

"It also states the people in the surrounding towns burned it down because of the plague."

"I knew you wouldn't believe me."

"You can say that again."

I added, "Not only that…but the change in my appearance is also due to visiting that town."

"What are you talking about? Your disheveled appearance is due to your abuse of alcohol, nothing else," said an angry Captain Bird, as he pounded his fist on the desktop to make his point.

"Captain, for some reason, once a person visits that shop or town, they start aging at an accelerated rate. I know all of this sounds crazy and off the wall, but please believe me."

"Zoolu, are you serious?"

"I'm not just saying this because I'm drunk. I'm telling the truth. If you don't believe *me*, ask the two eyewitness that also had the same thing happen to them."

"Where are they? I'd like to speak with them."

"Ah, they're in the hospital," I said softly, staring at the floor.

"Did you say hospital? What hospital?"

"I can't remember the name of the place, but it's on the south side of town," I replied, nervously chewing on another fingernail.

"Wait a minute. The only hospital on the south side is a mental institution. Don't tell me your eyewitnesses are patients at the mental institution?"

"Yes, but they were lucid and coherent. They were as normal as you or me."

"Well, I'm not sure you sound normal, anymore."

"Why is that, Captain?"

"You tell me that the reason you look like crap is due to visiting that town. A town that hasn't been around for over one hundred and thirty years or so. Isn't that right, Detective Zoolu?" he asked, as he stood up.

"Yes, Captain. You're right. The town burned down more than a hundred and thirty years ago. But somehow, it still exists today. And yes, I believe I caught some type of aging disease after visiting that town."

"Just listen to yourself, Detective. First you tell me that some evil entity had taken over your mind and body. And now you tell me that you've caught an aging disease from a town that doesn't exist. I think you need help. I also think you need some time off so you can get your drinking under control."

"Please, I'm fine. Really, Captain. I don't need any time off. Not right now, anyway."

"Zoolu, I believe you are having hallucinations or maybe you're going through the D.T.'s? I want you to make an appointment to see the company doctor. You've been working too hard lately. I think Detective Webber's disappearance has left you physically and emotionally drained."

"Please, don't do this to me, Captain."

"You really need to dry out. And you're suspended with pay, until further notice."

"You're going to ruin my career or what's left of it," I whined, as I tried to stand, but fell back into the chair.

"Zoolu, you've only yourself to blame. You are not to return to work until you have the approval of the company's psychiatrist and the medical doctor."

"Is that all, Captain?"

"No. Once you have their approval, then you will need mine. And if you give me any more lip, I'll think of some other things for you to comply with. So let's get your act together. Don't come back here until you're well. Is that understood, Detective Zoolu?"

I bowed my head in disgust, and embarrassment.

"Yes, sir. I understand perfectly."

"Good. Now, you may leave," said Captain Bird, waving me out of his office.

I slowly staggered to my feet and stumbled out the door. I was saddened by the fact that no one believed my story. But I was angry that I had been suspended and had to see a psychiatrist for telling the truth. But what could I do? I had been stopped for erratic driving. I had been caught while driving under the influence of alcohol. I suppose I could have lied to the officer and given him an excuse for my irrational behavior? But instead, I told the truth and nobody believed me. They thought I was making it all up. In short, they thought I was lying or just losing my mind. It was as simple as that.

What had I gotten myself into, I asked myself as I staggered out to the parking lot and into my car? The officer had it towed to the station for me. I just hoped another patrol unit wouldn't stop me. I would probably be arrested for drunk driving again? Even so, I decided to chance it and started the car. I had sobered up a little bit, but I was still inebriated.

While driving home I thought about what had just transpired over the last few hours. I felt angry and humiliated. I wanted to get home as quickly as possible and drink my troubles away. I wanted to stay drunk for a month. But first, I needed some food in my stomach. I figured I would stop at Gabriele's and order their specialty of the house, and my favorite, steak and cheese hoagies. They would serve as my breakfast, lunch and dinner. I could eat them any time of the day and had quite often. But not lately.

After a short ride, while constantly looking into my rear-view mirror for police cars, I arrived at the cafe. I parked the car without hitting any other vehicles then stumbled out of the car and up the stairs to the door of the cafe. When I entered through the front door, I noticed something was amiss. My favorite waitress, Bonnie, was on the telephone, but hung up immediately when she saw me enter.

"I'm glad you're here," said Bonnie, anxiously. "I've been trying to call you, but they said you had just left."

"Well, I'm here now," I said, while staggering over to the lunch counter. "What do you need?"

"You are investigating your partner's disappearance, aren't you?"

"I *was* investigating the case, but it's on hold for a few days." I left it at that, not wanting to reveal anything about my suspension. "Why, what's going on?"

"I don't really know what's going on? But, there is a lady in the back room lying down. She's resting now, but I think she needs your help."

"Why, what happened to her?" I asked as I followed Bonnie to the back room.

"I think she's been accosted by someone."

"Why do you say that?"

"Because I saw her walking in circles, outside the cafe. I walked outside and helped her into the restaurant. She was disoriented and incoherent, and she had blood running down the front of her blouse."

As we entered the back room I saw a meek, little lady dressed in buckskin clothing. Her left shoulder had been injured, but someone had bandaged the area. Julie, one of the other waitresses, was wiping her forehead with a wet washrag. The injured lady was muttering, somewhat incoherently, as Bonnie checked her shoulder wound.

I looked at the wound as Bonnie changed the bandage. It wasn't bad at all. The lady had a small, quarter-sized cut at the top of her shoulder, just above the collarbone. Bonnie took off the lady's blouse. I grabbed it and checked it out. It looked like the shirt was handmade from an animal hide. It was made with incredible craftsmanship.

I placed the shirt in a bag and placed it on the floor in a corner of the room. After Bonnie had cleaned the lady's wound, she used one of her work shirts to clothe the lady's body, then covered her with a heavy blanket. The lady wasn't too old. Maybe in her early thirties. She was a very pretty, petite woman. The two waitresses and I talked, while the injured woman rested on the couch.

"So what happened to her, Bonnie? Did she say anything?" I asked.

"Well, she muttered something, but I couldn't quite understand her."

"Why?"

"She kept mumbling about her wound. I guess she was in a lot of pain."

"Her wound isn't that bad," I told her. "How did she injure herself? Was she assaulted?"

"Remember when I asked you if you were still investigating your partner's disappearance?"

"Yeah. So?"

"Well, I think that's what happened to her husband. I think he's missing…but I'm not sure."

"Why do you say that?" I asked her.

"I couldn't understand the whole story," said Bonnie, after she lit a cigarette and took a deep drag.

"Why couldn't you understand her? Was she speaking in a foreign language?"

"No. She was speaking English, but talking irrationally."

"Well, tell me what she said."

"I don't know if you'll believe what I'm about to tell you," Bonnie said, nervously. "Because I don't think I believe the story she told me."

"So, what did she tell you?"

"I couldn't understand everything, but what I did understand is that her and her husband were at some party. I think they were at a party or going to a party."

But then Julie, the other waitress, interrupted her.

"It was the Madre Gras Ball."

"Oh, yeah," said Bonnie, after exhaling a large cloud of smoke from her cigarette. "It was a Madre Gras Ball. Her and her husband dressed up as Colonel Custer and Calamity Jane. I guess when they went to leave out the front door, something strange happened and her husband disappeared. Now, here's the weird part."

"What's that?" I asked.

"She said that her injured shoulder was caused by an arrow. That's about all I could get out of her. Then you arrived."

"Seeing as I don't have anything planned on my agenda right at this moment, I guess I'll stick around so I can ask her a few questions."

As the two waitresses and I continued our conversation, the injured lady suddenly sat up. She was startled to see us and had forgotten where she was.

"Hello, I'm Detective Zoolu. I'm here to help you," I told the injured and confused woman. "Can you tell me your name?"

After a few long seconds, she answered him in a high-pitched voice, sweat dripping off her forehead. "My name is Susan. Susan McCoy. How long have I been here?"

"You have been here for almost an hour," said Julie.

"Do you remember what happened to you?" I asked the dazed and frightened woman, kneeling next to her. "Where you came from? Where you were going? Do you remember anything?"

"I don't know? I'm so confused and mixed up. My husband. My husband. He's gone."

"Where did your husband go? Do you remember?" I asked.

She had to think for a minute, then said in a quiet and soft voice, "Everything seems so hazy and fuzzy. I'm very dizzy and lightheaded. I only remember a little bit of what happened."

"Just take your time, Mrs. McCoy," I said soothingly. "There's no hurry. Just tell us what happened."

"I don't know if I believe what I saw? I know you won't," she said, as she rolled her head from side to side.

"Don't worry about us. Just tell us the story like you saw it unfold. We won't say a word. We'll just sit back and listen, I promise." I patted her on her good shoulder and was waiting anxiously to hear her story.

"Could I have a glass of water please?" asked the wounded and frail woman.

"Sure," said Bonnie, as she retrieved a glass of water and handed it to the injured woman.

The lady drank nearly the whole glass of water in one gulp and then began her story.

"Well, I remember we were out driving in the country and we got into a big argument over money. I wanted to go to the Madre Gras party that our club was having and he wanted to stay home, because we couldn't afford the price of the tickets on our meager budget. But I wouldn't take *no*, for an answer."

"So, you went driving in the country. Do you remember what road you were driving on?" I asked.

She didn't know. "We were arguing so much, that my husband, who was driving, wasn't watching the road. I don't know how, but somehow we lost our way and found ourselves on this old, mountain road."

"Are you sure it was a mountain road? There aren't any mountains in this state," I reminded her.

"I know. That's why it was so strange. I thought we were driving on the main highway but I guess while we were arguing we somehow had taken a turn off."

"Why didn't you turn around if you knew you were lost?" I asked.

She replied that the road was too narrow to make a U-turn. "I mean, one minute we were driving on a highway and the next thing I knew, we were driving on a mountain road."

"Was the mountain road cement or asphalt?" I asked, hoping she wouldn't say dirt.

"No, it was a dirt road. A winding and narrow dirt road."

"So, what did you and your husband do next?"

"We couldn't make a U-turn, so my husband decided to follow the road, hoping it would lead us to a gas station so we could get directions to the main highway. My husband couldn't figure what he had done wrong. He didn't believe that he had somehow turned onto another road. So, we continued to drive up this long, winding mountain road."

"What were the weather conditions like in that area?" I asked.

"When we started out on our drive it was beautiful outside. But, nearly halfway up the mountain, the weather changed for the worse. It damn near picked up our car and threw it three feet into the air. We suddenly lost control of the car and our minds. It was incredible. It was as if we were in a trance," said the bewildered woman, after she had taken a sip of water.

"Mrs. McCoy, are you saying that you couldn't move any part of your body?" I asked.

"That's right. I was frozen like a Popsicle," she said, closing her eyes, as if she wanted to sleep.

I got up off my knees and pulled a chair close to the couch, then sat down on it. I waited and watched as the two waitresses helped make the slightly injured lady comfortable. They placed a small pillow under her neck and raised her feet onto a small table. I watched the face of the victim and tried to read her thoughts. I knew where she had been, but I waited for her to tell me. After five minutes or so of silence, we continued our conversation.

"Mrs. McCoy, you were telling us that you and your husband were driving up that mountain road. Please, continue?" I asked.

She said the weather continued to get worse by the minute. "The clouds turned as black as night, then a thick, misty fog clouded the sky. We could barely see out of the windshield. By the time we were going down the mountain, the car was being demolished by giant, balls of hail," recalled the woman, as she looked at the startled faces of the two waitresses, listening to her tale.

"Were you still in a trance?" I asked.

She nodded. "I had never seen or felt anything like that in my life. As the car rocked back and forth from the powerful winds and rain, and with the hail beating against the car, it sounded as if we were standing next to a shooting cannon being fired from a battleship. By the time we had gotten out of that crazy storm and neared the bottom of the mountain, we had finally broken out of our trance and could move our bodies again. When we had reached the bottom of that mountain, we found ourselves in a canyon and heading for a little town."

"So, when you came out on that canyon floor, you had the use of all of your faculties. Is that right, Mrs. McCoy?" I asked.

She said that once they reached the floor of the canyon, the weather cleared and they once again had control of our senses. "It was amazing.

Whatever had control of us had suddenly relinquished its power. It had even taken control of our car for a time."

I continued asking her questions. "So how long did it take you to reach the town?"

She stated that it the drive only took about five or ten minutes. Adding, "But when we arrived, the whole town was shut down."

"What do you mean, shut down?"

"The place was desolate. It reminded me of a ghost town. In fact, the only place that we could see to ask for directions was a place called the Costume Shop. So, we parked the car and decided to ask the people inside just where in the heck we were."

"Had you ever seen this town before?"

She shook her head and replied, "Heck no. The town looked like it had come out of an old, history book. It looked as though it didn't belong in the twentieth century, let alone the twenty-first. At first, we thought the town was deserted. There wasn't a soul around."

"You didn't see anyone else running around that town?" I asked.

"It sounds strange, doesn't it? We didn't see any other vehicles or any people roaming the street. I had an eerie feeling in the pit of my stomach. Something kept gnawing in the back of my mind."

"What was it?" I asked her.

"I'm not sure. I just felt very uneasy."

"So, you parked your car and then what did you and your husband do?"

"We entered the little shop to ask for directions."

"Who was there?"

"There was only this funny-looking, old man standing behind a small counter," she said, as she scratched her injured shoulder. "While I stared at the costumes my husband walked up to the counter to ask the old man a question." She whimpered.

"Take your time, Mrs. McCoy," I told her. "We called for an ambulance, so it should be here any minute. Go ahead and finish your story."

"Well, my husband was trying to get the directions from the old man, but instead, was talked into renting costumes for our Madre Gras Ball."

"Why didn't you just ignore the old man?"

"I don't know, something seemed to happen when the man behind the counter looked at me with those buggy eyes."

"What do you mean, Mrs. McCoy?"

"His eyes," she replied, staring into space, "looking through his thick eyeglasses, were magnified about ten times the normal size and he kept staring at me."

"It sounds like he has funny looking eyes, that's for sure. Did you like his costumes?" I asked her, knowing she did.

"Yes. He did have some mighty, beautiful costumes. They were all handmade and looked and felt like the real item."

"So, I take it you rented a costume?"

"Yes, I did. But only after my husband had picked out the costume of Colonel Custer, the Indian fighter."

"Which one did you pick out?" asked Bonnie, wiping the victim's forehead with a damp washrag.

"I picked out the Calamity Jane outfit," cried McCoy, scratching her shoulder wound. "It was handmade out of real deer hide. But now, it's ruined. The blouse is stained with my blood and so are the buckskin pants. The shirt also has a big rip in it at the shoulder from the arrow."

"Is this your costume?" I asked, holding up the bag that held her bloody shirt.

She nodded. "Yes. That's the shirt I was wearing."

"So what happened to your husband?"

"Well, when we decided on our costumes, we went into the back room, where there is a very small, one-person changing room. Hell, it's just a few blankets held up by a rope. But it worked."

"Yes, go ahead," I said, wanting her to finish the story before the paramedics arrived.

"Anyways, my husband changed into his costume first and then I changed into mine. We bundled our clothes into a neat pile and I handed them to the old man, sitting behind the counter, for safe keeping."

"Did he take them?"

"At first, that weird, little man really didn't want to hold on to them, but relinquished when my husband said he would take his business elsewhere. So he set our clothes behind the counter."

"When were you going to retrieve your clothes, if you didn't know how you got to the town in the first place?" I asked.

She thought for a minute and then answered, "We were going to pick them up when we returned the costumes. We didn't have to pay a cent for the costumes until we returned them. Plus, it was within our budget. We only had to pay for the rental of the costumes and we didn't have to leave a security deposit. The only rule we had to follow was to wear the costumes out of the shop."

"But how would you have gotten back to that town?"

"We would have asked that funny, little man for the directions. He was going to give us the directions to get home. But, before we left the shop the old man wanted to make sure we felt comfortable in our costumes."

"Why is that?" I asked.

"He told us that once a customer leaves with a costume that they couldn't exchange it for another. So, we agreed with his crazy rules."

"Did he ever give you the directions you needed?"

"Yes, he explained to my husband the correct way to get back onto the highway. So we thanked him and started on our way."

"Then you and your husband left wearing the costumes?"

"Yes."

I continued with my questioning. "So, Mrs. McCoy, when did you notice that your husband had disappeared?"

"My husband walked out of the shop first. When he opened the front door, all was normal. But just as he stepped outside of the shop, something mighty strange happened."

"What?" I asked, but knowing the answer.

"A bright, flash of white light blinded my eyes," she replied, not believing what she had seen. "I was so shocked and startled by the incident that I stepped back a few feet from the open door and stood frozen in terror, watching as my husband was surrounded by hundreds of union soldiers that were being attacked by thousands of hostile Indians."

"What were the soldiers doing? Were they shooting at the Indians?"

"The soldiers were fighting and standing their ground as the Indians massacred them."

"How long did this massacre take?"

"What seemed like hours, I believe, was really only a few seconds. But I was in a state of shock so I'm not sure. Bullets and arrows were flying from the Indian's weapons. Arrows even hit the front of the shop. One suddenly came through the open door and struck me in the shoulder."

"Mrs. McCoy, where were you standing when you got hit by that arrow?" I asked.

"I was standing right in the middle of the open door. I was standing, half in and half out. But when the arrow clipped my shoulder, it knocked me back into the shop and knocked me out of my trance."

"You really think you were in a trance?"

"Yes, I do. The hunchbacked, little, fat man had some type of hold on me."

"How do you know that all of this wasn't a dream? Maybe you were hypnotized?"

She shook her head, no, and continued with her story. "At first, I didn't realize I was hurt. But seconds later, I noticed a bloody arrow laying on the floor a few feet behind me. I suddenly felt a sharp, stinging pain in my upper, left shoulder. That's when I noticed I was bleeding."

"How much time went by when all this happened?" I asked.

"Like I said, it seemed like an hour, but I'm sure it was just a matter of seconds."

"What happened after you were struck by the arrow?"

"I stood frozen in time, watching the massacre. I saw all the dead soldiers, including my husband laying in an open field then one Indian woman came along and began poking a long, thin stick through my husband's ears and into his brain." She seemed mystified by her answer.

"How gross!" exclaimed Bonnie.

"Quiet girls. Let Mrs. McCoy finish telling her story," I said, motioning to them to keep their mouths shut. "Please, continue, Mrs. McCoy."

"I could hear the roar of the large crowd of victorious Indians, yelling and shouting with joy. When a few of those Indians saw me watching them, they began shooting more arrows at me."

"What happened next?" I asked.

"I shut the door, as fast as I could."

"What happened after you shut the door?"

"The second I shut that door, the shouting and yelling stopped. There was dead silence. Then, I remember feeling lightheaded. The room began to spin in circles and I guess, I must have passed out."

"For how long?"

She shrugged her shoulders. "I don't know how long I laid there, on that dirty floor. But I picked myself up and shook the dirt off my costume and felt my bleeding wound. For a second, I had forgotten what had transpired outside that shop. Then suddenly, I remembered. I opened the front door of that costume shop very slowly, and hoped another arrow wouldn't hit me. But, there was nothing."

"You mean your husband and all the other dead soldiers were gone?" I asked.

"Yes. The town was like it was when we had first arrived there."

"And how was that?"

"Desolate. Everything looked normal again. I wondered where my husband had gone, and all those dead soldiers and savage Indians? There wasn't any sign of them anywhere. I suddenly, felt sick to my stomach. I wanted to throw up. But I couldn't move. I was frozen in time and space. It was as if I was glued to the floor of the shop."

"Why do you think that happened?" I asked.

She shrugged her shoulders. "I guess I was too frightened to move. Then, suddenly, my body felt as though it was on fire. My forehead was hot and sweaty. My throat was dry and coarse. And my shoulder burned, as though someone had stuck me with a red, hot poker. And then my whole body burned, as though someone had dropped me into a blazing furnace. I started to sweat profusely and my body began to shake. The room started spinning again and I blacked out."

"How long did you black out this time?"

"I have no idea."

"What happened after you recovered from your black out?"

"I found myself standing outside this cafe and this darling girl helped me by letting me rest here, until I was strong enough to leave on my own," she said, as she smiled at Bonnie, the waitress that had helped her into the cafe.

"Well, the ambulance should be here shortly. The paramedics should be able to help you," I told her, trying to ease her mind. "They'll probably want to take you to the hospital so you can have your wound checked out. But, I wouldn't mention your story to anyone else, especially to a law enforcement official."

"Why not? I'm telling the truth."

"Believe me, they may not understand your story like I do."

"What should I tell them?"

"Just tell whoever asks, that you were attacked by masked hoodlums."

"What do I tell them about my injury?"

"Tell them that you injured your shoulder from a knife wielding thug during a mugging," I said, giving her an alibi and rational story. "But that it happened so fast that you didn't see your attacker."

"I just hope they believe me. Boy, I feel so tired and run down. I feel like I'm all used up."

"You look fine," I said, reassuring her.

"But I **would** like to know what happened to my husband. Did I really see him being murdered by all of those Indians? Is my husband really dead or was I just hallucinating?"

"How long has your husband's family lived in this area?" I asked her.

"His family goes back seven generations. They've always lived in this area, since his relatives came to this country from Ireland."

"When did they come here from Ireland?"

"My husband's relatives came to this country in the mid-seventeen hundreds. But I've never heard or seen anything like this before, except when my grandmother used to tell me a story about an old, strange town that was built on Indian land. But not just any Indian land, it was sacred land to those Indians."

"Are you talking about the Legend of Hollow Pass?" I asked.

"Yes."

"What did your grandmother tell you about that legend?" I asked, as the two waitresses gathered closer to the injured woman to listen to her story.

"The story goes that the townspeople of a little, mining town wanted to wipe out a nearby, large, Indian tribe."

"Why did they want to kill those Indians?"

"They were all witch doctors."

"So they killed them all?" I asked.

"Yes, but their bodies were never buried and their spirits are said to still be wandering the Earth. A couple of months after all the Indians were massacred…that little town and all the townspeople came down with some deadly disease."

"What kind of disease?" I asked.

"I think it was the plague. Anyway, the townspeople from the surrounding towns and villages, got together and decided to burn down the town, so the disease wouldn't spread."

"How did they catch the plague?"

"The people said it was the curse that the Indians had put on the town and its people for destroying their lives and families. Since then, legend has it, that every so often the evil witch doctors' spirits come and take some human lives for their own that were destroyed long ago."

"Is that what you believe, Mrs. McCoy?"

"I don't know what I believe."

"Why would the spirits from long ago, take the lives of these people today?" I asked.

"The legend states, that for each human the Indian spirits destroy, one Indian spirit is finally reunited with his loved ones somewhere in this vast universe. That's the superstitious legend that has been talked about for over a hundred years or more."

"Is that what you think happened to your husband?" I asked, looking deep into her eyes. "Do you think an Indian spirit took his soul?"

"I don't know if I do or not."

"You're sure that the hunchbacked, old man didn't hypnotize you?"

"He could have. I'm just so tired and confused right now, I don't know what to think."

That's when it hit me. I remembered her last name, McCoy. I remembered seeing and hearing that name. But where? When? Something in my head suddenly clicked. I came up with a new theory. But I wanted to make sure, before I said anything. In fact, I wasn't sure I would say anything even if I could, or my Captain may never let me come back to work.

But I was certain that I had found a logical explanation why all of these people were suddenly disappearing. Whether or not I could bring them back was a different story. But I was sure I was on the right path. But I needed to remember where I had heard the name, McCoy before. It was right on the tip of my tongue. But it just wouldn't come loose.

We stopped speaking for a few minutes, so everyone could catch their breath and relax while we waited for the ambulance to arrive. Nearly five minutes later, just as I was about to ask Mrs. McCoy another question, the paramedics entered the room and began treating the injured lady's wounded shoulder.

"What happened to her?" asked one of the paramedics, as he looked at the injured woman's shoulder wound.

"It looks to me like she cut her shoulder," I said, not wanting to tell them the real story.

The paramedics cleaned and redressed her wound then placed her onto a stretcher and into the waiting ambulance.

"Mrs. McCoy, I'll see you tomorrow at the hospital," I yelled.

A few seconds later, the ambulance quickly sped away.

I had half of the injured woman's costume in my hands. I figured I would visit the injured lady at the hospital the following morning and retrieve the pants. I wanted to have the costume analyzed at the forensic lab. I wanted the technicians to test and check the garment for the type of material and its age. That is, if the lab crew would do that for me. Especially, if they knew I had been suspended. So I had a lot of work to do.

After all of the excitement, I still hadn't eaten. I was totally famished. I was also in need of a drink. Susan McCoy's predicament had completely sobered me up.

I also wanted to visit the library to check out those three history books that I had glanced through before. Especially, the one that had the copy of the ghost town. I was sure I would find the answer in that book. I hoped I would, anyway. But it was too late to go there today. It would have to wait until tomorrow. I was hoping that I would find the answer to what I was looking for and that it would put my investigation that much farther ahead. I wanted to find a reasonable explanation for all of these strange occurrences.

The two waitresses and I walked back into the restaurant. I ordered my meal of two steak and cheese hoagie sandwiches. I only had ice water for my drink. I thanked Bonnie for calling me and thinking of me in her hour of need. But now that the excitement was over I decided to get back to work on my investigation.

But then, I remembered that I had been suspended and didn't have any investigation to work on anymore. I had gotten myself into quite a predicament and hoped I could get myself out of it. But this time I wanted more proof than just three, old, lead bullets and a deerskin costume to back up my irrational story. I was determined to find the proof I needed, even though I had been suspended. Too many people depended on me.

I finished eating my hoagies, left a big tip and headed for home. During my short ride, I thought only about my investigation and my stupid suspension. Now, I was sober once again. But within twenty minutes, I wouldn't be. I would be feeding my addiction to numb my feelings. I didn't care if I was suspended or not. I didn't care what Captain Bird had told me? I was still going to investigate my partner's disappearance. I could feel I was getting closer to an answer. I just had to be very discreet and not step on anyone's toes.

Once I had left the cafe, I had planned to return home, but headed for the hospital instead. I wanted to get the pants to Mrs. McCoy's costume. When I entered the hospital I went directly to the emergency room. Sure enough she was sitting up on a gurney as the doctor was stitching her wound. She was in a hospital gown and the pants to her costume were lying on a nearby chair. I quietly walked up to her and watched the doctor do his job.

"Excuse me, Mrs. McCoy," I interjected.

"Oh, it's you. Detective Zoolu, I believe," said Mrs. Susan McCoy, as she and the doctor turned to look at me.

"I didn't mean to interrupt anything, but I just wanted to pick up the rest of your costume. Is that all right with you, Mrs. McCoy?"

"Why do you want the costume?" she asked.

"I want to have it tested," I replied, trying to tell her as little as possible.

"Of course you may have the costume. But I want it back so I can return it to that crazy costume shop. That is, if I can find it again."

"Thank you," I said, as I grabbed the garment. "I'll leave you now, and let the doctor do his job."

I turned and left the room and headed for the hospital parking lot. I jumped into my car and headed for my home. It was definitely time for a drink or two or three. I would take Mrs. McCoy's costume with me in the morning and give it to the forensic lab for testing and carbon dating. But right now, all that was on my mind was a good, stiff drink.

I finally arrived at my place. I quickly parked the car and ran up the steps to the front door. Once inside, I couldn't get to that kitchen cabinet fast enough. I picked out a clean shot glass and an almost full bottle of twenty-year-old scotch, then danced into the living room.

I plopped my tired body onto the couch and began exercising my right arm. I drank shot after shot until I lost complete track of time. Then I must have passed out because that's the last thing I remembered. The next thing I knew, I had awakened out of my drunken stupor from the same nightmare that I'd been having night after night since I had started my partner's investigation.

Tonight I was more frightened than ever. I wanted to believe my dreams were trying to tell me something. But what? I looked at the clock and it was only three in the morning, so I shut my eyes and went back to sleep. But it wasn't long before that nightmare overtook my dreams once again.

I was suddenly back in that little shop of horrors. That little, hunchbacked, fat, old man was staring at me through his thick, coke-bottled eyeglasses, his human face had now turned into that of a grotesque gargoyle. I wasn't teasing him this time. The moment the little man noticed me, he jumped onto the counter and blew small fireballs out of his nostrils at me and then engulfed my body in fire rings. When my body burst into giant flames, the now grotesque gargoyle with hoofed feet, began inhaling and sucking my flaming body into his mouth. But this time, before he could completely swallow me, he spat me back out. I was a smoldering piece of meat, broiled to a burnt black color.

As I tried to shake the burning and smoldering ash from my charred body, that half man-half goat started snorting fireballs from his nostrils once again. His torment started all over again. I was darker than a piece of burnt toast. My hair was completely burnt off. My ears had been burned so bad that they had fallen off. One leg was burned off at the kneecap and my left forearm was burned to the bone.

But the ugly demon in my nightmare continued to spit more and more fireballs and fire rings at me. As I shook more and more black ash from my smoldering, burnt body, I had noticed the ash that had fallen onto the floor formed a small sentence. The letters spelled out the words: ***Jump Thru Door.*** That's all I had seen before a small breeze had blown the ash all over the shop. I wondered what my nightmare was trying to tell me.

I stayed frozen, afraid I would disintegrate if I moved. But the hunchbacked monster continued shooting fireballs at me. When he bombarded me with fire rings, I went up in a blaze of glory. Once again, the hoofed demon took a very deep breath. As he inhaled, he ingested my flaming body into his open mouth, again. This time he totally consumed me.

Just at that instant, I awoke in a cold sweat. I looked at the clock and it was time to get up. It was time for work. But then I realized I didn't have to go to work this morning. I was suspended. I thought about it for a few seconds, then fluffed up my pillows, shut my eyes and went back to sleep thinking about those three words from my nightmare.

CHAPTER 9

I finally awoke two hours later and with a terrible hangover. I still wanted to visit the library and forensic lab sometime today, hangover or not. I quickly washed and dressed, and ate a continental breakfast of toast, marmalade and hot, black coffee. My head continued to pound, like a badly tuned, twelve-cylinder motor. But that was nothing unusual to me.

When I finished my breakfast, I headed out the door and jumped into my car with Mrs. McCoy's costume in hand. Even though I had been suspended from my job I still had work to do on my partner's investigation, but I had to do it without Captain Bird finding out. He would most likely fire me.

I drove to the forensic lab first. I wanted to get that out of the way. It was nearly lunchtime, so most of the staff would be gone. Hopefully, I wouldn't be noticed. I arrived at the lab, but waited until I was certain there wasn't anyone hanging around outside. Because of the suspension I wasn't allowed on the premises. But this was important. If these garments were as old as I thought they were, it would answer a question or two.

I discreetly entered the medical examiner's building with the costume concealed in a brown paper bag. There was no one in sight. I went directly to the supervisor's office. Charlie Bell happened to be a very good friend of mine, so I knew he would help me. Luckily he was there eating his home-cooked lunch.

"How you doing, Charlie?" I asked, hoping he wouldn't turn his back on me.

"Pretty good. How's your investigation going?"

"Slow. Very slow," I said, wondering if he had heard I had been suspended.

"Have you got any good leads yet?"

"That's why I'm here today." I pulled the folded costume out of the paper bag and handed the garments to him.

"What are these?" asked the supervisor, as he looked over the costume.

"These are hopefully one piece of the puzzle, a big piece."

"What do you want done to them?"

"Check the age of the garments and tell me what this material is," I said, stroking the soft and heavy fabric.

"Okay, but I don't know when I'll have the report finished."

"Listen, when you do complete it, please don't send the report to my office."

"Why not? That's where I've always sent them before," said Mr. Bell, as he stuffed his mouth with food.

"They'll just lose it over there."

"So what do you want me to do, hang on to it?"

"Yes. I'll call you in a few days and pick it up myself. Also, I will need to return these garments to the owner, so please don't destroy them. The owner wants them back as soon as we are finished examining them. I would appreciate it if you keep this to yourself."

"Why is that?"

"I was supposed to be interviewing another witness today. I wasn't supposed to be here. So keep it under your hat. Okay?"

"No problem," said Charlie Bell, as he buried his head in his food. "I should have an answer for you in two days. Check with me then."

I turned and walked out to the parking lot and hopped into my car. I drove directly to the library and then went to the same book shelf as before. All three books were there. I grabbed them and took them to a corner desk. I quickly glanced through them until I found the correct page. It was the same page that I had photocopied before. But I had copied the picture, not any of its text.

Near the end of the page was the answer I was looking for. It listed some of the family names of the townspeople that had not only participated in both the extermination of the tribe of Indian witch doctors and the destruction of the town that the Indians had cursed over one hundred and thirty years ago but also the ones who had died from the plague.

There were over twenty names listed of families that had lived in three or four of the surrounding towns and villages during that period. I finally came to a name I recognized: McCoy, the family of Luke and Dottie McCoy. I presumed they were Susan McCoy's husband's great, great grandparents.

I looked to see if there were any other names that were the same as any of the people that had disappeared? I recognized a few other names: Saber, Kall, Dante and my partner's name, Webber. That was three out of the five or so people I had interviewed, plus my partner's name. It seemed the people that were involved in these disappearances had ancestors that either had something to do with burning down the town, or killing and dismembering the Indians or both. I wasn't positively certain that these people who had disappeared were related to these family names mentioned in the history book. But I was sure I was on the right track. I returned the books to the shelf and headed for my car.

It was nearly dinnertime, so I headed back to my house. During the ride home, my investigation wouldn't leave my thoughts. I had figured the forensic lab should have my analysis done on the costume in two days, just like the supervisor had told me. Once they had completed that task, I'd have them check out the three bullets that I had pulled out of the wooden panel from the front wall of the costume shop. I also wanted to return there to look for the arrow that had pierced Susan McCoy's shoulder.

Actually, I thought to myself, I shouldn't be investigating at all. If my Captain gets wind of it he will definitely fire me. So I had to be very discreet.

For the next few days I decided to stay away from that town and surrounding area. I decided to stay around the house and listen to the police scanner. I didn't have anything better to do than to sit and drink my blues away. That's exactly what I started doing. The minute I arrived at my place, I started exercising my right arm and thinking about my investigation.

I hadn't eaten since breakfast, but I wanted to drink instead of eat. I wanted to celebrate. I finally had some pertinent evidence to back up my crazy story. Just a few more pieces to the puzzle and I would win my respect back. I hoped so anyway.

But for now, I was suspended from my job. If any of my peers caught me investigating my partner's disappearance, I'd be looking for a new job.

So instead of worrying about the investigation, I thought about my health. The aging disease was still ravaging my body. I had to find a way to reverse it before it was too late. But what could I do? I wasn't a doctor. So to rid myself of these problems, I just drank my cares and troubles away.

I didn't eat and didn't sleep. I more or less passed out, listening to the police scanner and lying on my favorite couch. Every few hours I would wake up in a cold sweat as the same crazy nightmare overtook my dreams. This went on for two straight days. During those two days, I drank myself into oblivion, staying in a drunken stupor. I didn't eat at all during this time. The only thing that touched my mouth and stomach was liquor, twenty-year-old liquor. But soon my drinking binge would end because my case of scotch was nearly depleted.

I stayed inside the house drinking and feeling sorry for myself. I felt like a champion thoroughbred that couldn't race because of an injury. I felt terrible.

While I was doing nothing, I presumed Detective Matthew was enthusiastically investigating his missing person's case. But just three days after my Captain had suspended me I was shocked to see Detective Matthew standing at my front door. When I opened the door, he greeted me with a big smile, which quickly disappeared when he saw my disheveled appearance.

"Hello, Detective Zoolu," said Detective Matthew, his eyes looking over my aging and drunken body.

"Hello to you too."

"I was going to ask how you are doing. But I can see that you are ill. Ill hell, you look like death warmed over. In fact, you look like crap."

"Come on, now. I don't look that bad," I said, leaning against the wall so I wouldn't fall down.

"You look as though you've aged ten years since I last saw you."

"It must be the flu."

"If you say so."

So, what brings you out this way, Detective Matthew?"

"Well, aren't you going to invite me in?"

"I'm sorry. Please come in. Let's talk inside," I said, while directing him into the living room.

"Have you seen a doctor or specialist yet, like you said you were going to do if your problem got any worse?"

"No, not yet. I'm feeling better now."

"You sure don't look it," said Matthew, noticing all the empty liquor bottles scattered around the living room.

"Have a seat," I said, as Matthew threw my dirty clothes and newspapers out of the chair and onto the floor. "Excuse the mess, I haven't been myself lately."

"I can see that. What the heck has gotten into you?"

"Why? What do you mean?"

"It's only a few minutes after seven a.m. and already you're plastered to the gills. You look as though you've been on a drinking binge for a week."

"No, just a few days," I joked, as I lit a cigarette.

"What's your problem?"

"I have many!" I retorted, as I slouched deep in my couch, feeling nauseated and aching from a pounding headache. "Where would you like me to start?"

"Tell me another time. But first, let me tell you why I'm here."

Matthew watched in utter amazement and disbelief as I quickly poured myself a shot of scotch and drank it down.

"Please don't do that," Matthew pleaded. "You're killing yourself. Do you think you really need that drink so early in the morning?"

But I could see and feel his anguish. My flippant attitude and my reckless behavior saddened him. He wanted to help me, but he knew he couldn't.

"This is the elixir of life. It's the aphrodisiac of liquid dreams," I said, as I poured another shot of booze down my gullet, and watched as Detective Matthew bowed and shook his head in disbelief and disgust.

"Please, slow down with that stuff. Won't you?"

"You were saying?" I asked, ignoring his pleas and drinking another shot.

"You're disgusting."

"No, I'm drinking," I joked, as I toasted my glass into the air.

"I wish you would stop that."

"Why?"

"I can't talk to you when you're like this."

"Why, what do you want?"

"I stopped by your office today, but the officer at the front desk said you were off for the day due to an illness in the family."

"Then why did he send you here?" I asked him, getting drunker by the minute.

"I guess he presumed you were at home."

"How did you know where I lived?"

Matthew said he had gotten directions from the officer at the front desk and decided to stop by and talk with me about our investigations. "But I can see you're not up to it today."

"If you say so."

"It's true, isn't it? You are sick, aren't you? That's the reason that you aren't working today? Isn't it?"

"Well, I guess you can say I'm sick."

"What? Like sick from a disease?"

"I hope not."

"Then what?"

"I'm sick of all the hypocrisy in this world. Especially in our profession," I replied, slurring my words and accidentally spitting all over my guest.

"Are you feeling up for a little drive?"

"Where do you want to go?" I asked, and stopped drinking for a few minutes.

"If you're not too drunk I thought we might take a ride out to that town and I would follow behind you in my car. Do you want to go?"

"I don't think I'm in any shape to get behind a wheel of a car. I'd be an accident waiting to happen," I told him.

"We don't have to leave right this very minute. I will make us some coffee while you take a cold shower."

"You think that will help?"

"Yes, I do," answered Matthew. Adding, "When you have a pot or two of coffee into your system, along with that cold shower, that should sober you up enough to drive your car."

"Why do you want to go out there today?"

"I have a few questions I would like to ask that hunchbacked, old man that you and my witnesses have talked about so often."

"Why do I need to go? *You* know the way."

"I need you as my witness, listening to every word that's spoken. That's why I want you there with me."

"Believe me. I'd like to go with you, but I just can't."

"You're not chickening out, are you?" asked Matthew.

"Chickening out? That's the last excuse I would use. I guess they didn't tell you at the station," I said, in a sad and dejected voice.

"Tell me what? Tell me what, Detective Zoolu?"

"I was suspended a few days ago. If I'm caught investigating my partner's disappearance, I'll be looking for another job. Then I'd lose my pension. So I have to back off and keep a low profile."

"Heck, I didn't hear anything about that. Nobody mentioned that while I was visiting your station today."

"That's not unusual," I replied.

"What was the reason behind your suspension?"

"It's a long story."

"I have time."

"Well, Matthew, if you really want to know? All I did was tell the truth. But they didn't want to hear my story."

"What do you mean?"

"My Captain didn't understand my explanation of my partner's disappearance."

"You mean, they suspended you for just doing your job?"

"You could say that," I replied, hanging my head in disgust.

"I can't believe that. You had to do something that's worth suspending you for? What was it?"

"Captain Bird doesn't believe in these mysterious happenings. Hell, I didn't believe it at first either. But I'm really starting to."

"Did you tell him about that 'Legend of Hollow Pass'?"

I nodded and said, "I believe I mentioned something about it."

"What about that old man that owns the shop? I thought you suspected him."

"I do. I still believe that he had something to do with all these disappearances."

"But why were you suspended from your job?"

I slowly told him the reason. "Well, I guess I did do a rather stupid thing. I thought I had a good idea, but it turned out to be a big mistake."

"Why, what did you do?"

"You may have the same reaction to my explanation as my Captain had. In fact, you may not believe a word I say, but believe me, it's all true."

"Don't worry. I trust you. Just tell me what happened."

"Okay, you win. But please give me the benefit of doubt."

"I will. So what happened?" Matthew asked, anxiously.

I began telling him my reasoning behind my madness. "Well, I wanted to trick that spirit or entity that overpowers my being every time I drive to that mysterious area."

"What mysterious spirit are you talking about?"

"You'll find out what I mean when you visit the place. But anyway, I decided I would get stinking drunk before driving into that crazy area."

"Why in god's name would you want to do that?"

"You promise not to laugh or make fun of me?" I asked.

"I promise. Now why did you get drunk?"

"I didn't think that spirit could invade my drunken mind. But it turned out I was wrong. It had no effect on it at all."

"No kidding."

"But that's not the end of it," I told him.

"You mean there's more to your insanity?" asked Matthew.

"Much more. While I was in that shop, I actually saw someone disappear in a hail of gunfire."

"But you were drunk. You said so yourself."

"You're right. At first, I thought I was just hallucinating. But then, when I went outside to check out the area, I found three spent bullets in a wooden pane in the front of the building." I checked my pockets for the bag of bullets. "Here they are." I held them in front of Detective Matthew's face.

"Did you have them analyzed?" asked Matthew, as he checked out the spent bullets.

"Not yet. I'm having another piece of evidence checked out as we speak."

"Well, I can't say that I believe your story. But I do know that drinking and driving was a big mistake."

I had to agree. "Yeah, but that's not the whole story."

"There's more?" asked Matthew rather sarcastically.

"I saved the best part for last."

"All right let me hear it."

"When I was driving back towards the station, I was pulled over by a patrol unit. I told the police officer the story I just told you."

"You didn't."

"I did."

"What did the police officer do?"

"He got me in trouble. He drove me to the station and informed my Captain about my drinking. I was chastised and belittled. When I walked out of my Captain's office, I felt dehumanized and worthless. I felt I had let my whole department down," I said, toasting my empty shot glass into the air.

"Well now I see why you were suspended. What were you thinking?"

"I guess, you could say, I wasn't thinking."

Matthew decided to make the drive by himself. "I just hope your map is correct," he said. "I don't want to end up driving for three hours and find myself in another state. But I should be near the area in about two hours, right?"

"Yeah," I replied. "That's about right. You should run into that mountain road within two hours if you do the speed limit. But remember if you go out there, expect the unexpected. Throw the word, **_normal,_** out the window."

"What about that spirit that you told me about?"

I told him to fight it. Adding, "I know it will overpower you like it did me. So try and stay calm. It'll disappear in a short time. It may feel like hours, but it will only be minutes."

"Is that it? Is there anything else I should know?"

"Yeah! When you return to your precinct I wouldn't tell anyone about what you have seen or experienced. You may end up like me and all I did was tell the truth," I said, pouring another shot of scotch down my throat.

"If this crazy stuff really happens, that's why it's even more important that you go, too. So I have a witness to back up my story."

"I'm afraid they still wouldn't believe us."

"Why not?" he asked.

"They would say we were crazy. They are afraid to believe my story. But I haven't told you the reason behind it."

"So tell me," Matthew pleaded.

"Before I do, I want you to experience the phenomenon. Then, and only then, will we discuss our experience and talk about the next step in our investigations."

"I wish you would change your mind and follow me out there in your car."

"I really have to decline."

"Why?" whined Matthew.

"I'm going to stay away from that place for a few days. Right now, I'm waiting for a call from the forensic lab for the analysis report on my evidence, so I *can't* leave."

"Why can't they send the report to your office?"

"I have to pick up the analysis report at the lab. If they send it to my office, my Captain would fire me if he found out. So I have to be very careful."

"Well, maybe we'll go out there another time, hey?"

"It's possible. But, I can't say for sure one way or the other. I hope you can understand?"

"Okay," said Matthew as we walked to the front door. "I got my map and my gas tank is full. So I'm all set. I'll see you when I return."

"Okay. Drive careful," I told him, as he walked out the front door and stood on the porch.

He turned and gave me a stern warning. "Don't take this wrong, but you should slow down on your drinking. In fact, you should quit for a while and dry out. It's making you old before your time."

"Yeah. We'll talk about that when you return. I promise," I said, as I watched Detective Matthew walk to his car and drive away.

While I moped around the house, I made a phone call to the forensic lab. I wanted to find out if they had any information for me. It had been nearly three days and I hadn't heard anything about the costume yet. I finally got through to the supervisor.

"Hey Charlie. This is Detective Zoolu. Have you finished the analysis of the garments yet?"

"Yes. You won't believe what we have found. I did the test repeatedly to make sure my computations were correct. You wanted to know the age of these garments and what we found is beyond comprehension."

"How old are they?" I asked him.

"These clothes are nearly a hundred and fifty years old."

"Are you positive? Are they really that old?"

"We carbon dated the two garments four different times. These clothes are handmade from deerskin hides. The craftsmanship is exceptional and exquisite."

"Yes, I know that."

"Except for the small tear in the shoulder area of the shirt and the blood stains, these clothes could sell at auction for thousands of dollars."

"They are worth that much?" I asked.

"Yes, they couldn't be made like this today. I don't think we could duplicate their work."

"Really, Charlie? They're made that well?"

"It's really fine quality and craftsmanship. I am very impressed. Where in the heck did you find these?"

"I don't want to say just yet."

"This is a rare find. Let me know if you get anymore. I might have a buyer."

"Great. I will do that, Charlie. In fact, I will be at the lab in a day or so to pick up the garments."

"They are all ready for you. Come any time."

"Oh yeah, I have three bullets I want you to analyze. I forgot to give them to you the other day. But would you take a look at them for me and call me when you're finished testing them?"

"Will do. But tell me. Is it true that you were suspended?"

"Who told you that?" I asked him.

"I don't know," he replied. "Everyone is talking about it. They're saying you saw ghosts or something. I don't get into all that gossip. But I hope you are doing all right?"

"Yeah, thanks. I'll see you sometime tomorrow," I said, then hung up the phone.

Suddenly, my thoughts jumped from the spent bullets to Detective Matthew. I was worried about him. I knew he was in for the shock of his life. I just hoped he could handle it. I don't know why, but I just couldn't stop thinking about him. I was really afraid for his life.

The longer I stayed in the house, the more agitated I became. I couldn't sit idly by any longer. I decided to take a chance and drive my car. I felt Detective Matthew's life and well-being was worth the risk. But first I wanted to drive to the forensic lab and pick up the costume. I wanted to take it back to the costume shop and barter it to the hunchback for some answers to all of these disappearances.

Before I left the house I soaked my head in the sink with very cold ice water. That was the best and quickest way to sober myself up. Five minutes later, I was driving towards the forensic lab. Even though the cold water made me alert, I was still quite inebriated. I drove as cautiously as could be. Unfortunately, my reflexes were slower than usual. I nearly caused two different accidents in the 5-minute drive to the lab.

I quickly parked my car and stumbled to the front door. Just as I was about to enter the building, Captain Bird came around the corner and headed right towards me. I wanted to disappear before he noticed me, but it was too late. He saw me. He gave me an angry look and walked directly to me.

"Detective Zoolu," snapped Bird, getting right into my face. "What the hell are you doing here? Do you want to be fired?"

"No, sir."

"Why shouldn't I fire you? You know you aren't allowed on the premises while you're on suspension."

"I know, sir."

"But you still disregard my orders. What have you got to say for yourself?"

"Sir, I know I'm not supposed to be on city property but the forensic lab telephoned and wanted me to pick up some evidence that had been left in their possession. They wanted me to get it out of their hair and return it to the proper owner. The grieving, victim's partner wanted the items returned. So, I volunteered to return them to their rightful owner." I knew I was lying to him but I had no choice. Unless I wanted to get fired.

"Well. Get the evidence and return it. I don't want to see you near this place again. At least not until your suspension has been lifted. Is that understood, Detective Zoolu?"

"Yes, sir. Thank you, sir. It won't happen again. I promise," I said, reaching out to shake his hand, but he declined.

My Captain ignored me. He was standing within inches of my intoxicated body and I knew he could smell the alcohol on my breath.

"Have you been drinking? You smell like a damn brewery," snapped Captain Bird.

"What do you want me to tell you, Captain?"

"You're not driving, are you?"

I didn't say a word. I was too embarrassed to speak. But he could tell I was guilty.

"What's wrong with you, Detective? Do you want to cause an accident?"

"Captain, I was going out of my mind being locked up all day with nothing to do."

"You get whatever it is that you have to get. But I will tell you this. You drive directly back to your place and stay there and sober up, before you deliver anything to anyone. Do you hear me, Detective Zoolu?"

"Yes sir, I do," I said, staring at the ground.

"You are representing our police department, not a bar. Do you understand me?" barked my Captain, as he scolded me in front of my peers.

"Yes, I do."

"If I ever see you in this condition again, on suspension or not, you will be fired, immediately. Is that understood?"

"Yes, I understand. Thank you, sir. I won't let it happen again. I promise. I won't let you down," I said, as I quickly staggered past my Captain and into the medical examiner's building.

I stumbled to the forensic lab looking for the supervisor. But the room was empty. I looked in another room or two before I finally found him looking into a microscope.

"Hey, Charlie. How are you doing?" I asked, as I patted him on his shoulder.

"What the heck are you doing around here today? Your Captain was just here a few minutes ago. If he catches you, he'll have your head on a platter. I wasn't expecting you until tomorrow. What the heck changed your mind?"

"Actually, I had another place I wanted to visit once I left this place. But speaking of the Captain, I did run into him."

"What did he say to you?"

"I was lucky he didn't fire me. So I can't stay too long. But before I leave, I have something else I would like you to analyze, when you get the time." I pulled the bag of spent bullets out of my pants pocket and handed them to him.

"What are these?" asked Charlie, as he inspected the spent, lead bullets.

"What do they look like? I want you to test and analyze these bullets just as you did the costume."

"You want me to tell you what material they are made out of?"

"Well, kind of. I want to know the age of the bullets. I want to know what size they are and what material used to make them. Is it pure lead or what? I know bullets made a hundred years ago were made with slightly less impure materials than today's bullets."

"Will do," Bell promised. "It might take me a day or so before I have the report complete."

"That's fine. But remember, telephone my home when you're finished. Don't send the report to my office. I don't want to give the Captain an excuse to fire me. Would you do that for me?"

"Sure. No, problem. Just do me one favor?"

"What's that?"

"Just clean up your act. You look like hell. You have really gone downhill in the last couple of weeks. I can't believe how fast you have deteriorated."

"Don't worry about me, I'm fine."

"I'm telling you," Bell said sternly. "If you don't slow down with your drinking, it's going to kill you. It looks like it's already started to take its toll."

"Thanks. I know you're not telling me anything I don't already know. But there is something else you don't understand and no one will until I have the proof I need."

"Yeah, what's that?"

"I can't say right now, Charlie. But listen. Don't worry about me. I have everything under control. Believe me."

"If you say so. Just take care of yourself," he said, as he went back to looking into his microscope.

I turned and stumbled out of the room with the costume under my arm.

I staggered to my car and sat in it for a few minutes. I debated whether I should risk it and drive out to that crazy, mysterious town? I was still very worried about Detective Matthew, but I was also worried about what Captain Bird would do to me if he ever found out.

Finally, I came to the conclusion that if I could do it and get through it, so could he. If I returned alive and well, so should he. But I would never forgive myself if something did happen to him and I might have been able to save him.

But I gave up the idea to go after him. I guess I thought more about losing my job than about Detective Matthew. I came to the conclusion that he was a big boy and could handle the situation, whatever it might be. So, I pushed the thought out of my mind and drove towards my place. I decided I would return the costume another time. But I would still use it as leverage against the hunchback. If he wanted the costume back, he would have to answer some of my questions.

Dejected, somber and against my better judgment, I returned home. I drove cautiously from the forensic lab to my place. I was afraid that Captain Bird would have a patrol car follow me. I was right. I noticed a unit following about ten car lengths behind me. They slowed as they passed my driveway and checked to see if I was at my place of residence? I waved to them as the patrol car passed by.

I grabbed the costume and headed for my front door. The minute I entered, I walked hurriedly to the kitchen. But this time things were different. I didn't reach for my bottle of scotch. I decided to stay sober for the rest of the day. I wanted to be sober and in good enough shape to drive. Just in case something out of the ordinary happened.

But I was too bored to just sit and do nothing but twiddle my thumbs. I was very fidgety and uneasy. Every minute I thought about not drinking, it seemed like an hour. My body perspired profusely. I became agitated very easily and couldn't sit still. I was very nervous and anxious thinking about Detective Matthew.

I nearly changed my mind a number of times to drive out to that town. If nothing else just to see how Matthew was doing.

Only three hours had passed since I had last checked the clock, but it had seemed like thirty hours. Time was completely out of kilt to me. By the time evening rolled around I was a nervous wreck.

It had been over eleven hours since I last saw Matthew. Now I was really getting worried. He promised to return to my place and tell me what transpired from his visit to that weird town. I was so worried that I began getting ready to drive to that town. Even though it was getting late and was already quite dark, I felt that Detective Matthew needed my help.

I grabbed the keys to my car from the kitchen counter and put on my jacket. I didn't care about my own future and the repercussions from my actions. I was only thinking about my friend's life. Just as I opened the front door and stepped outside, I bumped into what felt like a brick wall. When I grabbed the arm of the person lying on the ground I was shocked, but happy to see Detective Matthew. He was out of breath and had actually seemed frightened. I thought maybe I had scared him when I bumped into him? I helped him brush off the dirt from his clothes as we walked into my abode.

"Detective Matthew, I was just coming to look for you," I told him as we walked into the living room and took our seats. "You were gone a very long time. What the heck were you doing out there? Digging up the desert looking for dead bodies?"

"Not quite," he said. "But I'll tell you one thing about that area. I've never experienced anything like that in my entire life. It's a phenomenon that's unexplainable. I'm shaking like a leaf." He held up his shaking hands.

"Calm down. Take it easy. Just sit back and relax for a few minutes. Take a couple of deep breaths."

I could tell Matthew had visited that costume shop. His face had looked as though it had aged ten years. I didn't want to say anything to him about it. But I knew I would have to tell him eventually. He would find out anyway. He just couldn't sit still. He would stand up, pace three or four steps and then sit down again. But that lasted only a few minutes until he moved from chair to chair, racing from one side of the room to the other. I couldn't get him to calm down. He was a nervous wreck.

"Detective Zoolu, how do you handle it? I think I'm having a nervous breakdown," said Matthew, as he wiped off his sweaty forehead.

"Come on now. Snap out of it. Tell me what happened," I said, as I reached over and shook him by his shoulders.

"Well, at least I know now that the map was drawn correctly. I found that town fairly easily. Getting there, however, was somewhat of a challenge. But that mountain just appeared out of nowhere."

"Didn't I tell you to expect the unexpected?"

"I couldn't believe it. Thank god, there weren't any other cars around or I would have smashed into them."

"Why?"

"That mountain appeared so fast that it startled me and I nearly lost control of my car. I thought I was having a heart attack."

"Did you see any other people around that town?"

"Not at first. In fact, I was the only person in that town besides that old man in the shop. However, I did see that little boy, afterwards, that you've talked about. Oh, and I also saw an old Indian man."

"What did you think of them?"

"They are just as strange as the rest of the place," replied Matthew, finally settling down and beginning to relax, as best he could under the circumstances.

"Did you run into horrible weather?"

"Did I? You can say that again. But let me tell you what happened."

"I'm sorry. Just start from the beginning. Take your time. We have all night," I said, sitting back in my couch.

After taking a few deep breaths, Matthew began telling me his story. "I left your place and followed the map as best I could. I kept checking my watch until I approached two hours. There wasn't another car or person in sight. But suddenly, out of nowhere, I felt myself climbing up a steep incline and I felt the change in altitude. A thick blanket of fog covered my car completely. Then a sharp, torrent wind began blowing my car all over the road. Did you have the same experience?"

"I told you before. Expect the unexpected. Please, continue with your story," I said, not wanting to tell him my experience until he told me his.

"Luckily, there weren't any other vehicles around or I would have probably been killed? I looked for the turn at the top of the mountain, but something took control of my body."

"When did you feel something had control of your body? Was it before you reached the top of the mountain or after?" I asked him.

"It hit me not long after the mountain appeared. It seemed the weather turned into a torrential downpour and at the same time, something seemed to take control of my body and car."

"What did this invisible force do to you?"

"I tried to turn my head and I couldn't move. I couldn't move my arms or legs. I couldn't move a muscle. I wanted to fight that strange power, but something in my head kept telling me not to. Whatever it was that had a spell over me sure didn't keep me from being frightened out of my mind. It sure didn't have control of my bladder, either, because I pissed my damn pants."

"What about your car? Did you have control over it?"

"No, I didn't," said Matthew, biting his fingernails. "The car steered itself. But the weather really had control of it."

"What do you mean?"

"The weather pushed the car up and down the mountain. Then the wind would lift the car a couple of inches into the air and throw it ten feet forward. Somehow the car stayed on the road. I thought I was a goner a few times when the wind pushed the car close to the edge of the ravine."

"Did it rain or hail, while you were driving on that mountain road?"

"Yes, it did. But I'm getting way ahead of myself. Please, don't interrupt me. I'm too upset and confused as it is."

"I'm sorry. Go ahead. Start over." I leaned back into my couch and got comfortable as he began telling me about his experience in a desert town that didn't exist.

"So anyway, the hundred mile an hour winds kept pushing my car down that winding, mountain road, but never in a straight line and I couldn't do anything about it. Then, just when I neared the bottom of the mountain, a big, gust of wind, literally, picked up my car."

"Were you still under the control of that invisible force or did you have control of your faculties?"

"It still had complete control of me. I take that back. It didn't have control of my bladder," said Matthew.

"How do you know?"

"When that gust of wind picked up the car I thought it was going to crush me against the side of the mountain. But instead it turned my car away from it, in midair, then dropped it right on top of a huge figure walking in the middle of the road. That's when I pissed my pants."

"Then that invisible force must have released its hold on you at that moment."

"It could have. But I wasn't thinking about it when that gust of wind crushed that thing under my car."

"Your car landed on someone?"

"Yeah. The second I landed on the canyon floor, I felt that invisible power leave my body. So, I got out of the car to check to see if that thing was still alive."

"What was it?" I asked.

"I'm not sure. When I looked there was nothing there. But I could have sworn my car had landed on a grizzly bear or some type of animal with long, dirty, furry, brown hair. It must have been a hallucination because I didn't see it anywhere."

"I told you to expect the unexpected. What did you do when you saw there wasn't anyone under your car?"

"I continued to drive towards that town. Then about one hundred yards ahead me I saw that giant, hairy figure walking on the side of the road."

"Was it the same thing that you thought your car had landed on?" I asked.

"Yep. When it noticed my car, it turned and looked right at me. That's when I could see that it was just some giant, old man."

"Was he an old Indian man?"

"At first I didn't know. He could have been an Indian. I never had the chance to ask him. Every time I got within ten feet of him, he would suddenly disappear right before my eyes. I told myself it was just a mirage. But then a few seconds later, he was on the side of the road hitchhiking. So I stopped the car to see what he wanted? That's when I saw for the first time that the figure was that of a giant, old Indian man."

"What did the Indian want?"

"He asked for a ride into town and I obliged him," said Matthew, his body still shaking and sweaty.

"I've picked him up too. That guy's really a character. Isn't he?"

"Please, I'll lose my thought if you keep interrupting me. Let me finish my story. This is important to me. I think I'm losing my mind."

"I'm sorry. Continue," I said, lighting a cigarette.

"Like I was saying. This giant Indian was so huge he could barely fit in my car. Even with my front seat all the way back, the Indian's knees were still touching the windshield. He must have been nearly eight feet tall and five hundred pounds. He was mammoth."

"His name is Wallahoo Cecil," I told him.

"When I first saw him on the road, I thought he was a big, grizzly bear or a big, mammoth elephant. One thing was for sure, he was big. But he was also mysterious."

"Why do you say that?"

"When he learned I was going to see the man at the costume shop, he told me to turn around and leave the area," exclaimed Matthew.

"Did he give you a reason?"

"He wouldn't tell me why even though he too was also going to visit the costume shop."

"How do you know that?" I asked.

"He had a costume to sell. He said it was a dress made for a queen that represented the eleventh century. Some of the things he said, I couldn't quite understand, though."

"Like what?"

"He mentioned that he was over two hundred years old and that his family had been in this area for over two thousand years. I wasn't sure about that part of the conversation?"

"What else did he tell you?" I asked, anxiously waiting to hear his answer.

"He also mentioned that the old man that managed the costume shop was also a very, very old man."

"How old is he?"

"When I asked him the old man's age, he said he was also over two hundred years old. But that old Indian seemed senile to me. I didn't believe him at all."

"Why is that?"

"I believe he was just trying to frighten me, and he was doing a pretty good job. He mentioned something about that area being overrun with evil spirits and unholy demons."

"He's quite a character, isn't he?" I opined.

"I'll say this, he was one mysterious man. He started telling me about a cannibalistic Indian tribe that was massacred, butchered and sold as buffalo meat to unsuspecting visitors and townspeople."

"That sounds like the 'Legend of Hollow Pass'."

"I don't know, he was never able to finish the story."

"Why?"

"We had arrived at the costume shop."

"Did you both enter the costume shop together?" I asked.

"No," replied Matthew.

"Why not?"

"We both got out of the car at the same time, and I heard the passenger door shut, but when I looked in his direction, he wasn't there."

"You mean he left in a puff of smoke?"

"He couldn't have walked away or I would have seen him. I ran all around the car and looked in every direction I could, but he had disappeared. I quickly went into the costume shop thinking he went there before I got out of the car."

"Did he?"

"I heard both car doors slam shut nearly at the same time. He couldn't have walked past me that fast?"

"I told you to expect the unexpected," I said. "Was he in the shop?"

"No. When I entered the costume shop, I looked around the room but he wasn't there either. The only person in that shop was a hunchbacked, old, fat man with eyeglasses that were three-inches thick."

"That's him."

"His eyeglasses magnified his eyes about thirty times normal size. He was a very odd looking character."

"Did you talk with him?"

Matthew nodded. "I asked him if he had seen an old, giant, Indian man come into his shop."

"What did he say?"

"He said that the only person he saw come into his shop in the last five hours was me and only me."

"Was he lying?"

Matthew shrugged and said, "I was so dazed and confused, I couldn't even think straight. I didn't know what was happening to me? I thought I was losing my mind."

"Did you ever find out the truth from him?" I asked.

"I began a little conversation with the man. I was trying to size him up. He was a real fruitcake."

"What did you talk about?"

"We talked about many different things. But when I mentioned that the Policeman's Costume Ball was being held a few days from now he tried to talk me into renting one of his costumes."

"I take it you didn't rent one?"

"You're right," Matthew replied. "I wouldn't take the bait. I just ignored him and changed the subject."

"What did you talk about? Did you ask him about the missing people?"

"Every time I brought up the subject about people disappearing, he would also change the subject. When I asked him about his family, he told me they had been in these parts for over three hundred years. I nearly got him when I pointed to the photo on the wall of him standing outside of his costume shop and congratulated him for taking such a good picture."

"What did he say to that?"

"At first he thanked me. But then a few seconds later, when he realized I knew that the photo was taken back during the Civil War, he changed his tune. He became evasive. Saying, oh, you mean that picture. Then he pointed to the same picture as I did and said, 'oh, that's my great, great, great grandfather. I just happen to look like him'. But he didn't sound too convincing or believable."

"Why not?"

"After the weird things that I had experienced and saw or didn't see, everything seemed unbelievable. I was having a hard time distinguishing between fact and fiction."

"I told you to expect the unexpected," I reminded him.

"It was as if I was turned upside down and right side up," said Matthew, wiping the sweat from his brow. "My brain was coming unglued."

"What do you mean?"

"There were times when I thought I saw his face change into a demonic being. I was either hallucinating or losing my mind? I couldn't decide which. However, I wasn't able to witness any disappearances while I was there due to the lack of customers."

"Is that when you left and returned here?"

"No. I began a barrage of questions. But I soon became frustrated by the man's insistence of snubbing my questions and always changing the subject."

"Why, what was on his mind?"

Matthew said that he kept talking about the Policeman's Costume Ball. Adding, "As I tried asking him my questions, I also walked around his shop and inspected it for any type of evidence that might help in my investigation. When I walked by the front door, I opened it to get some fresh air and that's when I noticed a small, dirty-looking boy. He looked about nine or ten years old."

"He must have been the same boy that I had seen. Did you speak with him?"

"Not at that time. I stuck my head out of the open door to see where he had gone. But just as quickly, he had disappeared.

"What do you mean by disappear? How did he disappear?" I asked, lighting a cigarette.

"Not in a puff of smoke, but around a corner of one of the other dilapidated, wooden buildings."

"Oh."

"I decided then that I would talk to that kid before I left that crazy and weird town."

"Did you talk with him?"

"That's what took me so long. I sat in my car waiting for that little boy to show up again. Which he did. But again, I'm getting ahead of myself. As I was checking the shop's costumes near the back wall, that huge, old Indian man walked into the shop. I had to wipe my eyes to make sure I wasn't dreaming or hallucinating."

"Were you?" I asked.

"No I wasn't. I walked near him, close enough to hear him breathing. But I still wasn't satisfied so I accidentally bumped into him ever so slightly. Then I pinched myself to make sure I wasn't dreaming."

"What was the old Indian doing there?"

"He handed two different costumes across the counter to the hunchback. He seemed very happy, 'cause he had a smile on his face."

"What kind of costumes were they?"

"When the old man held them up to the light," replied Matthew, wiping his sweaty brow with his handkerchief. "I could see that one was a gladiator's costume and the other was a big, green, ruffled and frilly dress.

It looked like something that would have been made for a queen or princess. I'm sure it was a costume of royalty."

"What happened next?" I asked, anxiously waiting to hear his answer.

"When the hunchback was satisfied, he handed the giant Indian some money. I couldn't see the exact amount, but there were a number of large bills that had changed hands."

"How do you know how much money changed hands? You just got through saying that you didn't see the exact amount."

"When one of the bills fell to the floor, I bent down to retrieve it."

"How large was the bill?"

"I'm not sure?"

"Why not?" I asked.

"At the same time that I picked up the bill I bumped into one of the clothed mannequins and knocked it to the floor. I handed the bill to the Indian, then returned to pick up the mannequin. When I turned around, after I had picked up the mannequin, the Indian was gone."

"He disappeared too?"

"I guess he did. He was nowhere around. He couldn't have walked away that quickly. He just disappeared right in front of my eyes, once again."

"In a puff of smoke?"

"No," he replied. "I mean one second he was in that shop and the next second he was gone."

"So what happened next?"

"I ran to the front door, opened it and looked outside. Nothing. Not a soul around. He had disappeared in a wink of an eye. My head suddenly became dizzy and faint and I had to lean against the building to catch my breath and gather my senses."

"That place does that to a person."

"Yes, it does," Matthew replied. "But just as I closed the shop door behind me I saw out of the corner of my eye that little boy again."

"So, what did you do?"

"I wanted to talk with him, so I quickly turned and opened the door. I jumped out onto the steps of the building and yelled out to him, but he wasn't there. When I saw him an instant before, he was walking across the dirt street."

"So maybe he turned a corner or was hidden by one of those buildings?"

He shook his head, no, saying, "I opened that door just as it closed, so it was impossible for him to get across that street that quickly. It was utterly impossible. But yet, he wasn't anywhere in sight. I had to pinch myself to make sure I wasn't dreaming. I thought for sure I was losing my mind."

"I told you," I said, but was quickly interrupted.

"To expect the unexpected. I know, you've told me already," said Matthew.

"So, what did you do next?"

"I stepped back into the shop and asked that hunchback where everyone was disappearing too?"

"What did he say to that?"

"He didn't answer," Matthew replied. "I asked him where that little boy went to. Again, he didn't answer. When I kept badgering him with question after question, he came back with a question."

"What question?"

"He kept egging me on to rent one of his costumes for the ball. But I refused to answer his question just like he had been refusing to answer mine."

"So, what did the old man do then?" I asked him.

"He made comments about my mind and my eyes."

"And then what?"

"I became annoyed by his personal attacks about my eyesight. That was his excuse for my unusual questions. He kept insisting that I should see a good doctor for my hallucinations."

"You shouldn't have let him get under your skin."

He continued, adding, "I became even more frustrated and angry at his refusal to acknowledge the presence of the giant Indian or the little boy."

"He did?"

"Yes. He even denied buying the two costumes that I had seen the Indian hand him. He even held them up to the light. That's when I saw what type of costumes they were."

"What did the old man say to that?" I asked.

"He kept insisting I was a lunatic," he replied, adding, "After interviewing him for more than two hours, I gave up trying to converse with him."

"Is that when you decided to leave?"

"No. I went outside and sat in my car."

"Why? Were you pouting?"

"Please, give me a break," snapped Matthew.

"Then what were you doing?"

He thought for a minute and said, "At first I just sat thinking about my investigation and what I should do next. But then, I figured I would wait around to see if any customers would show up or if the Indian or little boy would come back so I could talk to them."

"Did they?"

"I waited and waited until I fell asleep. When I awoke I looked at my watch, but it wasn't working. I figured I had been in that town for nearly six hours. When I was getting ready to start my car, I'll be damned if that little boy didn't walk in front of it."

"What did you do then?" I asked, waiting to hear his answer.

"What do you think I did? I jumped out of my car and yelled to him. He stopped in his tracks, then turned and looked at me."

"What did you say to him?"

"I told him I just wanted to ask him a couple of questions. He agreed, so we got into my car. I got in the driver's side, he got in the passenger's side."

"What did this boy look like?"

"He was a very small, meek boy. He couldn't have been more than four feet tall and must have only weighed about sixty pounds. He had shaggy, long, black hair and looked as though he hadn't bathed in weeks."

"Yep. That was the same kid I had seen," I told him.

"His clothes were old and worn. He had on a dirty T-shirt that at one time had been a white color that had now turned a spotty brown. He was very quiet and shy. He didn't say a word. He only nodded or shook his head. At first, I thought he was a deaf mute. But I soon found out differently. He told me a story that was really unbelievable."

"How unbelievable could it have been after what you had just witnessed at that place?" I asked.

"You're absolutely right. I don't want to repeat my story to anyone else, but you. Even now, I don't think I believe the kid. It just sounds too far-fetched," said Matthew, finally taking a break to get a glass of water for his dry mouth and sore throat.

"I was wondering when you would give me a chance to speak."

"Just look at me, I'm shaking like a leaf," he said, showing me his shaking hands.

"Take a few deep breaths and relax."

"Hey, instead of water, how about giving me a shot of your scotch. I think I deserve a drink after what I just went through."

"Sure. Why not? Now you know what I've been through," I said, as I poured him a drink.

He quickly drank it down, but I thought it was going to come right back up just as fast. He began coughing and jumping up and down. Then he handed me his shot glass.

"Can I have another?" he asked, his hands still shaking as I poured him another shot of scotch.

While I was pouring, I noticed he was looking at himself in a mirror. I could see that he was noticing a change in his appearance. I did. I knew he had caught the aging disease. I didn't tell him about it before he left for the town because I wasn't sure if it would happen to him just by entering that crazy costume shop. I didn't want to believe it. I chose not to believe it. That's the reason I was drinking so much lately. Now I wondered if Matthew was going to follow in my footsteps. I really hoped not. He walked back to the couch and grabbed his glass of scotch, then sat back in his chair.

"Do you notice anything different about me?" Matthew asked.

"No. Why do you ask?" I replied, not wanting to make him aware of the fact that he may have the aging disease, too.

"I don't really know? My face just looks a little different. Hell, maybe it's all in my mind? Just like that hunchbacked, old man said."

I was anxious to hear what he had to say about the boy and mentioned it to him. "You didn't finish telling me about the conversation you had with the boy. What did the kid have to say, anything of importance?"

"Gee, I don't know where to start."

"Start at the beginning," I said, as I watched him gag on his drink.

"Let me have another drink," he said, holding out his glass.

"Are you sure you need it?"

"Yes. I'm sure," he replied, as I filled his glass.

"Please, continue with your story."

Once he had finished his drink he began telling me the conversation with the boy. "I told the boy I was investigating a friend's disappearance. I explained to him that I thought the old man had something to do with it. I also told him about other suspicious disappearances."

"What else did you tell the kid?"

He thought for a few seconds, then said, "I mentioned the fact that all the evidence pointed to this costume shop and its owner, but that we needed proof. I asked him if he knew anything about these disappearances or had any information that would help in my investigation."

"Anything else?"

"I also asked him how he was involved with the hunchback."

"What did he say?" I asked.

"He said he worked for him. Now get this. When I asked him how long he had worked for the old man? You know what his answer was?" Matthew asked me, sipping his fourth shot of scotch.

"I give up."

"He said he had been working for the old man for over one hundred and thirty years. I said that would make him over one hundred and thirty years old."

"What did he say?"

"He agreed. He said he was one hundred and thirty nine."

"What was he doing for that old man?"

Matthew told me that he had been retrieving the worn costumes from his customers.

"What did you say?"

He shrugged and replied, "I didn't say too much. I just listened to his story. I did interrupt him one time."

"For what?"

"I showed him a photo of the person that had disappeared and asked him if he had ever seen him before. He nodded, affirmatively."

"Where did he see him?"

"At the costume shop," replied Matthew. "But it was quite a long time ago. I asked why he was the one to collect the costumes."

"What did the kid say?"

"He said he was the witness."

"Witness? What did he mean by that?" I asked him.

"He said he was one of the first children that was killed. He wouldn't tell me how. But he did say it was a wicked, evil death. I tried to pry it out of him, but he was adamant. He refused to expand on his explanation."

"What else did he say about that crazy place?"

"He explained to me how this area was sacred ground to the Indian people. That it had been destroyed along with the tribe of witch doctors and medicine men. This was a very special tribe that had a gateway to the gods. But many people were afraid of them. They didn't understand their ways."

"So, what happened? This sounds like the 'Legend of Hollow Pass'," I opined.

"The townspeople of a nearby town thought the Indian tribe was evil and the Indian tribe thought the townspeople were evil. They antagonized each other until it got out of hand."

"So, what happened?" I asked, wanting to see if his answer was the same as I had heard.

He told me that many of the townspeople from the surrounding towns got together and raided the tribe of medicine men. Adding, "They were literally slaughtered in their sleep."

"That's the story of the 'Legend of Hollow Pass'."

"Yeah, but there's more."

"Well, let's hear it."

"The townspeople didn't just massacre those Indians. They were even more disrespectful to the gods and cut up the bodies into little pieces, then fed them to unsuspecting travelers."

"I don't think that was part of the legend."

"When they killed those Indians," Matthew explained, "their souls were never allowed to join the universal heavens. Their spirits were condemned to live here on earth until their debt was repaid to the gods."

Suddenly, a bright light went off in my head. "So that's why people are disappearing," I said.

"The boy said that could be the very reason why these people were disappearing from this area. The spirits were collecting the souls of the descendants of their murderers. Then and only then would their spirits be allowed to float freely throughout the universe."

"What did you say to that?"

"Nothing," Matthew replied. "I just let the boy speak. I didn't say a word. He was talking enough for the both of us. So, he continued on with his unbelievable story. He told me he had been retrieving costumes for over a century. I finally asked him how old the giant Indian was."

"What did he say? Did he know who you were talking about?" I asked.

"He knew exactly who I was talking about. He told me that the Indian was his father and was even older than the hunchbacked, old man."

"And how old is that?"

"He wouldn't say. Only that his father was older than the man at the costume shop. He has the responsibility of repairing and making costumes. The boy said that most of the costumes in the shop were produced by his father."

"What did you ask him about the missing people?"

Matthew replied, "I asked the boy why many of the victims' partners ended up going insane? He told me that anyone who was supposed to go through the portal and doesn't, succumbs to a deadly disease."

"What deadly disease is this?" I asked.

"They end up growing old before their time and it eats their brain from the inside out. They usually die within a few years, but they wish they had died long before that. I asked him what the hunchback had to do with this place and he told me that he was the caretaker."

"Caretaker. Caretaker of what?"

Matthew said the hunchback had been one of the people that had helped cut up the Indian bodies into little pieces and then sold them to unsuspecting travelers. Adding, "Now he is paying his debt to the gods for taking part in the massacre. If you look at the picture on the wall behind the counter, you'll see a man standing in front of the costume shop during the eighteen-sixties."

"Yes, I know. Who is the man?" I asked, anxiously awaiting the answer.

"That man in the picture is the same man sitting behind the counter in the costume shop,"

"I thought so. But what else did you ask the boy?"

Matthew said he asked him how many more bodies were needed before the gods would be satisfied.

"What did he say?"

"He refused to tell me. I don't think he knows. However, he did have more to say."

I asked him about the portal. "What is that?"

"I'm not sure," Matthew replied. "But I also asked him if he knew why the weather was so strange and crazy in that mountain range?"

"Did he tell you?" I asked him.

"Yeah. He told me the demons and angry spirits try to destroy anyone who comes to this town."

"Did he say how they arrive there?"

"He did. He said we are picked by the spirits. We are drawn to the area and then that mountain appears and it's the spirits that take control of our being and car. But the gods come to the rescue. They right the demons wrong. The boy maintained that the gods directed the car to the costume shop. He told me that the gods were responsible for keeping the car from plunging two thousand feet to the canyon floor or smashing into the side of the mountain."

"And how did they do that?"

"By reaching out and grabbing it as it flies through the air," replied Matthew. "Then gently placing the car safely back on the road. The boy said the gods and the spirits did all this, so they could get their revenge. I told him that the gods didn't want the demons to kill their enemies, but that the spirits themselves wanted to do the job. He agreed with me."

"Boy, I think I need another drink," I exclaimed.

"Can I have another drink, too? My body and mind are finally feeling numb. I don't drink very often, but what I went through today I think it's time to start."

"You better take it easy," I said, as I poured him another shot of scotch, which he drank just as fast. "Don't overdo it. If you intend to drive home tonight you better slow down your drinking. You're pretty well soaked to the gills now."

"I'm just trying to numb the senses. But you're right, I better not drink anymore tonight," said Matthew, looking at his watch. "It's getting pretty late and I still have a long drive ahead of me. If you have any coffee on, I'll gladly have a cup before I hit the road."

"Sure thing. I'll get you a cup. You like cream and sugar in your coffee, don't you?"

"You got it."

I walked into the kitchen, retrieved two cups of hot coffee and handed one to Matthew.

"Watch it, it's very hot," I said, as I sat back down on the couch to listen to what else he had to say.

"Do you remember the lady I had asked you to interview for me?" asked Matthew.

"Yes I do. Mrs. Kall, the lady at the nuthouse."

"Well, I showed the boy her photo," said Matthew, sipping his hot coffee, "and he remembered seeing her at the costume shop too. He told me that he had retrieved her husband's gangster outfit and his weapons. The funny thing about that is, I never mentioned what costume the guy had chosen. But the boy was absolutely correct. I think he wore the John Dillinger costume."

"But you don't know for sure, though, do you?"

"No. I know it was a gangster outfit, though. But just as the boy started explaining about the mysterious vortex we enter to arrive at this crazy town, that old Indian man walked slowly past the front of my vehicle and interrupted our conversation."

"So what happened?"

"When the boy noticed that it was his father that had just walked by, he quickly opened the passenger door of the car and jumped out, then ran to him. They were hugging each other as I left the vehicle. When I turned to walk towards them, they both just up and vanished right before my eyes. Just puff, and they were gone."

"Now do you believe me?" I asked him with pleading eyes.

Matthew shivered and said, "I had never seen anything like it in my life. I thought I was dreaming. That's when I jumped back into the car and drove back to your place. I couldn't get here fast enough. I went through the same weather that I had first experienced, but this time it was hailing large, walnut-sized ice balls. They nearly destroyed my automobile."

"I know. Look what it did to my car. It's a wreck."

Matthew continued with his story. "But before I had reached that mountainous area, I thought I had seen the boy and old Indian man walking on the side of the road, heading in the same direction as me."

"Was it them?" I asked.

"I don't know? I was never able to catch up to them."

"Why not?"

"I don't know why," said Matthew, sipping his coffee. "I wish I had the answer. I'll tell you one thing, I had one hell of a weird day today. Never in my life has anything like this ever happened to me before."

"So Matthew, do you really believe what you're saying?"

"Hell, I don't know? That's why I'm talking with you about it. You're the only person I can speak with rationally about this subject. You have experienced this strange phenomenon too. Haven't you?"

"I sure have," I told him. "When I told my commander and chief, he suspended me for it. I still need some hard evidence so I can throw it in my Captain's face and make him eat his words."

"Well, I think we are on the right track," exclaimed Matthew. "We are getting closer and closer to the truth. I can feel it."

"I *know* we're on the right track. But we have to come up with a plan to trick the hunchback into revealing his secrets to us?"

"How do we do that?"

"That's what we have to think about. If we put our heads together, we should be able to outsmart him."

"Except that we are dealing with spirits, gods and demons," exclaimed Matthew, wiping his sweaty forehead with his handkerchief. "Listen to what I'm saying. If I told this to anyone else, especially my peers, they would carry me to the nuthouse themselves."

"I know what you mean. We are going to have to do this on our own. I have already jeopardized my career. There is no use for you to jeopardize yours."

Matthew nodded and said, "You're absolutely right. But right now, I better get going. It's getting late. I need to get some rest and think about a plan of attack. I probably won't be around here for the next few days. I should be back either by the end of the week or the beginning of next week."

"Why is that?" I asked.

"I have a few chores to do that I have been neglecting," replied Matthew, as he finished his coffee and stood up to gather his senses and get his balance. "It will also give me time to dwell on our situation."

"Can you drive?"

Matthew nodded. "I guess I'm sober enough to drive. But I'm still blind drunk from the experience I had today." He began walking towards the front door.

"I hear that," I said, as I stood up and walked to him.

He continued speaking but with a slight slur. "If anything of importance comes up or if there is an emergency and you need my help, don't hesitate to contact me. You can telephone my station or cell phone. You have the numbers, don't you?"

"I sure do," I told him. Adding, "So, for the next couple of days put your thinking cap on and see if you can come up with some good ideas to penetrate that mysterious area. I'll do the same. But tonight, just drive safely. I need you to be my witness and you are no good to me dead." With that said, I watched him walk out the door, get in his car and drive away.

Once again I was alone. I wondered what I would do with all my free time. I went back into the living room and started drinking again. It seemed to help me concentrate on my problems. I wondered how much older Detective Matthew would look by the time he returned. These and many other questions were running rampant through my mind. I also wondered how much longer I would be on suspension. I was supposed to get the approval from the company's psychiatrist, but I hadn't even made an appointment to see him yet. I continued to drink as I dwelled on my problems. Ten drinks later, I was sleeping soundly. Again, I had passed out on the couch.

CHAPTER 10

I had again awakened in the middle of the night perspiring profusely. My dream had been overrun by demons. The monster in my nightmare had destroyed my beautiful dream. Basically, it had been the same nightmare that I had been having since I had begun this investigation. I was again consumed by fire rings that had been blown by that beast behind the counter of that costume shop.

The burnt ash from my smoldering body again spelled the words: "***Go thru door***". Those were the exact words that had come to me in my last nightmare. Something or someone was trying to tell me something, but I couldn't understand what?

I continued to be driven by that nightmare. Each time I fell back to sleep, I would awaken in a cold sweat from that same nightmare. But each time I had that awful dream, the demons would multiply. First, two demonic beings, then four, then eight. Finally, after I had awakened for the fourth time, morning had arrived so I decided to stay awake.

But it had been a long night. I needed two big pots of coffee just to keep my eyes open. Even though I didn't have to go to work, I still wanted to continue the investigation of my partner's disappearance. But due to my Captain's threat to fire me, I would have to be very discreet.

I nursed my hangover while I ate a small breakfast of toast, jam and coffee. I listened to my police scanner from morning till night. I was constantly bored staying indoors, so I decided to return to the library and read more about the town and its people. I had also wanted to read about that crazy legend: The "Legend of Hollow Pass". Also, I wanted to see if my name or my friend's name had been mentioned in any of the history books that I had glanced through before. I was certain that Detective Matthew and I had the aging disease. I had been hoping one of the books would have the secret to the words that I had seen in my nightmare: "***Go thru door***".

I also wanted to interview the two eyewitnesses from the mental institution again. Now that I knew more about that mysterious area, they may be able to tell me something of importance to help in my investigation. I wanted to talk to them about this so-called portal or vortex. Also, I wanted to find out if they knew anything about the "Legend of Hollow Pass". Many of the things I'd seen so far were directly out of the "Legend". But how could I prove it? That was my problem.

Right now, however, I was bored. I wanted to do anything other than stay at home. When I stayed inside, all I wanted to do was drink and listen to the police scanner that kept me in contact with my profession. I needed to come up with a good idea to trick the hunchback into giving up his secrets to the spirits and the gods. I needed, desperately, to find a way to stop or reverse the aging disease. I knew four or five people right off hand I could think of, that could benefit from reversing the dreaded disease or whatever it was that was slowly aging our bodies and eating away at our brains until there was nothing left. It was my responsibility to find the answers.

So I quickly dressed and set out for the library. I still had to be very discreet. If my Captain even thought I was working on my investigation, he would have my head. In fact, before I left the house, I made an appointment with the shrink for three o'clock that afternoon.

I had a little over four hours before I had to visit the psychiatrist, and wondered what I was going to tell him. I had to be careful when speaking to this man or I possibly could end up in that nut house too.

Finally, I was sitting behind the wheel of my car and driving towards the library. Once there, I went directly to the same shelf as before. The books were still there. I retrieved them and walked to another section: "Legends". I picked out what I thought was the correct book and carried all four books to a corner desk. I sat down and began reading where I had left off before.

I turned to the paragraph about the townspeople that had joined in the massacre of the Indian tribe. I read the list of names, but the ones I was most interested in weren't there. But then I found out why? This was a partial list of the townspeople from a small town south of the area. There were four or five different towns that had taken part: Not only in the massacre, but also in the torching of the dreaded, diseased town.

I continued to read more and more pages from the book. Finally, on the tenth page, I found one part of the answer I had been looking for. I had noticed another name listed that I had been familiar with. This time, the name was related to mine. That's why I had become involved in this crazy, ghost story. My ancestors had been involved from a town north of the mysterious area. They had not only helped torch the diseased town that was filled with the plague, but they had also helped in the massacre of the evil, Indian tribe. Reading that really frightened me. I wondered what other surprises the spirits and gods had for me?

I quickly discarded those negative thoughts. I tried to tell myself to only think positive thoughts if I wanted to beat these demons, and reverse its curse on the area. But how?

A few pages later, I had found another piece to the jigsaw puzzle. It mentioned a doctor of a town east of the area who had been the one that had recognized the dreaded disease that had been killing the residents of that mysterious town. Working long, hard hours at his research lab, he was able to find the strain of virus and isolate it.

Evidently, the townspeople had been their own worst enemy. They had become infected from the human meat they had sold to unsuspecting travelers. Their greed for money had been their worst enemy. The doctor's last name that had uncovered that disease in his laboratory was Matthew. I was sure that he had been the ancestor of Detective J. Matthew. I believed that had been the reason Detective Matthew had been mixed up in all of this madness and ungodly phenomenon. That was the only logical reason I could think of that answered the question of why he had been involved in this game of torture and lunacy by the spirits and the gods. If you could call it logical?

Maybe Matthew had come up with a different reason? I don't know? The doctor himself had been the first person that had set fire to the buildings in that diseased town during the Civil War days. Now one of his descendants was paying the price for the doctor's past actions.

I had made a much more precise list of names than the previous one I haphazardly threw together. I now had found more than twenty names of participants that had been connected to that mysterious area. I wondered how many more innocent people had to disappear before the gods would be satisfied.

I had hoped these books, including the one about 'legends', would somehow have the answers. I continued to read for a few more hours. Although I hadn't found out any more pertinent information, I was satisfied with what I had learned.

I had photocopied a number of pages to review and read at a later time. I wanted to think about the text and study its message. Maybe I would have to read between the lines for the answers that I needed? But now it was time for me to return home and get ready for my appointment with the shrink. I wanted to do whatever was necessary to get my suspension lifted as quickly as possible.

When I returned home, I still had over an hour before I had to leave for my appointment. I was very anxious and nervous about my meeting with the psychiatrist. I wanted everything to go well without getting myself into deeper trouble with my Captain.

I was so nervous my whole body quivered from head to toe. My whole being was shaking. Giant Goosebumps popped up all over my body. I wanted desperately to take a drink but I withstood the aggravation and temptation of my addiction. For once, my willpower won a decisive victory over my controlling addiction to alcohol.

I perspired profusely as the alcohol seeped out of my pores and soaked into my clothing. But I refused to give in to the demons of my addiction. Feeling sickly every second of every minute from my past abuse of alcohol, I quickly gulped down a hot cup of black coffee and started walking towards the front door. But just as I reached to open the door, the telephone rang. I turned and walked to the living room to answer it.

"Hello, I'm in a hurry. What do you need?" I snapped.

"Yes, Detective Zoolu. I'm a lab assistant and I'm calling for the forensic lab. Your analysis report is complete. Do you want it sent to your office or would you like to pick it up?"

"I'll pick it up later this afternoon. It will probably be after working hours so I'd appreciate it if you'd leave it on the supervisor's desk."

"Will do. It'll be there waiting for you," said the lab assistant, then hanging up the phone.

I did also and then walked out the front door. I drove directly to the psychiatrist's office. I had five minutes to spare by the time I arrived at his office. I was the only person in the room. There weren't any other patients or even a secretary, only a sign-in sheet sitting on a desk. So I quickly signed in and waited patiently, but nervously, in the waiting room until the psychiatrist came out of his office and introduced himself.

"Hello. I'm Dr. Franklin. I assume you're Detective Zoolu," he said, as I stood to shake his hand.

"Yes, I'm your three o'clock appointment. I hope you will give me the okay to go back to work."

"Well, let's see if we can do something about that," said Dr. Franklin, as he walked into his office while I followed close behind. "Please have a seat and let's see if we can get to the root of your problem." We both plopped into our chairs.

I watched as the psychiatrist sat in his big leather chair reading my medical report. I was feeling very uncomfortable in his presence. I felt that this appointment was a mistake and unnecessary. My drinking may have gotten me into trouble, but I had been sent here for telling the truth.

"Is that my file you're reading?" I asked, just to break the silence of the room.

"Yes it is," Dr. Franklin replied. "I also have the report from your Captain. It seems he's very worried about your mysterious behavior."

"What's wrong with my behavior?"

He stated that I had a total lack of responsibility for my actions. He went on. "The report states that since you began the investigation of your partner's disappearance you are close to going over the edge. Is this true?" he asked, as he tried to see into my psyche.

"I don't think so."

"It also states that your drinking is interfering with your job? Is this also true?"

I shook my head, answering, "Well, no, to both questions. I don't think I've gone over the edge and no, I don't think my drinking has interfered with my work. I will admit that I sometimes do have some stupid ideas that haven't worked out quite as I had planned. But to say I've gone over the edge, no I don't believe I have."

"Tell me about your idea that you deemed stupid," asked Dr. Franklin, as he began writing in his little notebook. "Why do you put yourself down, like that?"

"When I explain it, you may not understand?"

"Try me."

I shrugged. "Okay, you asked for it. I have been investigating my partner's disappearance for the past couple of weeks and some very mysterious things have been happening. I've uncovered some mighty strange evidence."

"Such as?"

"You may not believe it and I don't know if I totally believe it either, but I'm not the only person to experience this phenomenon."

"Oh, who else has experienced it?" asked the doc.

I explained to him that I had been working with another detective from another city that is also investigating some strange disappearances. "He will verify what I am telling you. It involves a strange town and its surrounding area," I said, as I pulled the photo and newspaper article out of my pocket and showed them to him.

"What is this?" he asked, looking at the photo of the deserted town, then grabbed the article and read it.

"That's the place that is behind all of these strange disappearances. I know it sounds ridiculous and crazy, but it's the truth."

"But the article states that this town had been burned down to get rid of the plague," said the psychiatrist, as he continued writing in his little notebook. "I don't understand how this could have anything to do with anyone's disappearance."

"Well, let's see if I can put it in perspective without sounding like a nut case." I took a deep breath and began explaining the phenomenon. "There is a town in that same area, right now, believe it or not. It's the same exact town that's seen in that photo you have sitting in front of you and the one that burned down during the Civil War." I sat nervously watching the reaction in his face.

"Let me get this straight. You say that you have seen and visited this town that burned down more than one hundred and thirty years ago? asked Dr. Franklin, holding up the photo in front of me. "You actually believe this?"

"Now hold on a minute," I snapped. "I knew I shouldn't have said a word about this. It makes me sound like I'm completely out of my mind and an utter idiot. But, I'm not. There is a reasonable explanation to these disappearances. Well, not reasonable, but logical. Well, not logical, but I do believe I know the reason."

"And what's the reason?"

"Have you ever heard of the 'Legend of Hollow Pass'?"

He nodded, saying, "I suppose I've heard something about it, why?"

I explained to him that it had something to do with an Indian tribe that the inhabitants of the town massacred. Adding, "Then the town's inhabitants became infected with a dreaded disease called the plague. This is all common knowledge. It's written in black and white in our history books. The people that were involved in the massacre are directly related to the people who are disappearing now."

"Why is that?"

I remained silent for a few seconds, and looked him straight into his eyes, then said, "It's their descendants that are disappearing. In fact, I have a list of names that I copied out of one of the history books from the library." I pulled out another page of the book that I had photocopied and handed it to him.

"You really believe this story about this town and its inhabitants? You actually believe in this 'Legend of Hollow Pass'?"

"Yes, I do."

"Even if I give you the benefit of doubt, it's still a hard pill to swallow. So tell me, where do all these people disappear too?" asked the doc, peering out from behind his little notebook.

I shrugged. "I'm not sure? But I believe the missing people were payment for the Indian souls that had been massacred by the townspeople. I have found that the people who have disappeared were related to people that took part in the massacre and or burning of the town. The names in the book correlate with the names of the victims. I'm sure of it."

The psychiatrist gave me a look of bewilderment while continuing to write in his little notebook.

"And who are taking these innocent people?" he asked.

"The spirits of the dead Indians."

"You really and truly believe that?"

"Yes, I do."

"Now then, Detective Zoolu, when did you start having these delusions?" he asked, looking at me with questioning eyes.

I gave him a disgusting look and became angry. "You think I'm having delusions? Everything, I've told you is the gospel truth. I've even showed you in black and white that the names of the townspeople and the names of the victims are connected. But yet, you think I'm having delusions. That's typical.   I guess, I'll have to bring Detective Matthew to my next appointment so he can verify my statements."

"Please, don't be angry with me. I'm trying to understand. Just be patient and bear with me."

"I'm sorry if I get upset, Doc. But I'm not a mental case. I'm telling you exactly what happened to me and a lot of other people. Believe me, I thought I was losing my mind at one time too. But through my investigation, I've learned and witnessed many weird things."

"Such as? Give me an example."

"Before I say another word about that strange place, I want another Detective here that has experienced the same things as I have concerning that crazy town. I could tell you much more if I wasn't so afraid to open up to you. But you have my life in your hands."

"Why do you say that?"

"I want to get back to work. But I need your approval before my Captain will allow me back on the squad. That's why."

"Enough about that town and its spirits," barked Dr. Franklin, peering from behind his notebook. "Tell me, when did you start drinking more than usual? Do you drink every day and are you alone when you drink?"

"I will admit, I have been drinking much more than usual since I started this investigation. But I feel I can control it. If you are asking me if I'm an alcoholic, I would say, *yes*."

"Why do you say that?"

I leaned back in my chair and said, "I drink alcohol every day and I drink alone. If that constitutes an alcoholic, then I'm definitely one. But that doesn't mean that I don't know the difference between reality and fiction? Don't you think I know how my story sounds?"

"Why? How does it sound?"

"Doc, I wouldn't have believed it either if the phenomenon hadn't happened to me. But it has happened to me. I'm sorry it has. But I can't do anything about that now. I will do whatever it takes to get back to my job."

"I'm all for that," he replied. "Let's see if we can control your drinking habit and then we'll see how much progress we have accomplished? I'm sure we'll have you back to work in no time." He looked in his appointment book. "I'll see you this same time the first of the week. That's Monday at three o'clock."

"Fine. I'll try and get my friend to come with me so he can verify my delusions," I said, sarcastically.

"That's right. You did say that you knew another detective that has had the same experience, didn't you? Let me ask you, is *he* a heavy drinker, also?"

"As a matter of fact, he hardly drinks at all. But you will be able to ask him that question yourself next week."

"Yes, I will. But we want to concentrate on your problems. I'm hoping that once we have your drinking under control, your delusions, excuse me, your experience might not seem the same to you as before? I'm hoping, you'll be your old self."

"Whatever you say, Doc."

"Very good. I'll see you next week then," said Dr. Franklin, as he shook my hand and walked me out of his office and to the elevators in the hall.

"Thanks for your time, Doc. I'll see you next week," I said, as I entered the elevator and rode it to the basement garage.

I drove my car directly to the forensic lab to pick up the ballistics report on the bullets I had found in the wooden building. It was well past closing time, but I still had to be discreet and not let anyone see me on the premises, especially Captain Bird.

I arrived at the forensic lab without being seen. I quietly crept into the supervisor's office and found the ballistics report sitting on the desk. I picked it up and walked out of the building to the parking lot. I then hopped into my car and drove straight home. I was anxious to read the report. I was hoping the evidence would somehow support my story.

The minute I walked into my abode, I went directly to my kitchen cabinet. I had been waiting all day to have a drink, and boy did I need one now. I poured three quick shots of scotch and drank them just as fast. I grabbed the bottle and glass and walked into the living room. I fell onto the couch and began drinking as I glanced over the ballistics reports. I noticed that there was one report for each bullet.

The first report stated that two of the bullets were carbon dated to be over one hundred and thirty years old. They were used in old western rifles, like the Winchester. The other bullet was used in machine guns; the type that was made in the early twenties, during the Al Capone days. That bullet was found to be nearly seventy years old. Each bullet was tested four different times.

Now I had some real evidence to show my doubters. But I had a dilemma. I had pulled the bullets out of a wall of a building that wasn't supposed to exist. And the bullets were real, not some delusion of my mind. I wondered how my superiors would respond once I showed them my evidence. Would they just dismiss my evidence outright? I really didn't care. I was sure they would listen to me when they heard two detectives telling the same crazy story.

Before long, I passed out again on my favorite couch. I awoke time and time again to my demonic nightmare and each time found myself inside that costume shop with that hunchbacked, old man. He would jump out from behind his little cubicle, stomp his cloven hoofs and blow fire rings from his mouth. The flaming fire rings would encircle my being until I was a smoldering, burnt pile of ash. Suddenly, the door opened and the wind blew my ashes throughout the shop and into the open sky. And at that moment, I awakened in a cold sweat frightened out of my mind. I tried to fight it but I couldn't shake it loose. It was also taking its toll on my body. I stayed in a drunken stupor for three straight days until that following Monday.

I had hoped that I would have heard from Detective Matthew by now, so he could come with me to my appointment with the psychiatrist. It was well past two o'clock and I still hadn't heard from him. I only had a half an hour before my appointment. With only ten minutes left, I decided to leave for my doctor's appointment. Just as I was walking down my steps, Detective Matthew was walking towards me.

"Hey, you finally made it. I need you to come with me," I said, pushing him towards my car.

"Man, you look like death warmed over. Have you been on a drinking binge?" asked Matthew.

"Don't ask."

"Where are we headed to?" he asked, as we hopped into my car and drove away.

"You'll see when we get there. Why don't you read these reports while you're relaxing," I said, handing him the ballistics report on the bullets and the costume.

"What are they?" Matthew asked.

"Read them. They might help you in your own investigation. I finally have the evidence I need to help prove my story. All I need is this evidence and your eyewitness testimony to back me up. A few more pieces of solid evidence wouldn't hurt either."

After a ten-minute drive, we entered my doctor's parking lot, parked the car, and then headed into the building for my appointment with the psychiatrist. When we entered his office, the room was empty, once again. We were the only people there. I still hadn't told Matthew where we were or why we were there? He was eagerly reading the ballistics reports as I waited for Dr. Franklin. I wondered how the doctor would react to my friend's story of that mysterious town. I was actually anxious for him to hear Detective Matthew's story. From that, I was hoping he would lift my suspension so I could go back to work and complete my investigation.

I still hadn't told the psychiatrist about the aging disease. And I wondered if the doctor would notice my inebriated state. I hoped not. But my body had that stinking, perspired, alcoholic odor that had seeped out of my pores. But, I didn't really care. Now I had an eyewitness, who was an honest hard-working detective.

I wasn't relying on testimony from a patient in the nut house, but rather a bona fide city employee and law enforcement official. I was sure the doctor would have to listen to my story no matter how unbelievable it might sound. I also had those ballistics reports and the evidence. What more would the psychiatrist need to make a logical judgment? Then I could throw it in my Captain's face and say: "I told you so."

It was ten minutes past three. The doctor was late. I was so nervous and anxious to get this appointment over with, I thought I would pee my pants. Detective Matthew wasn't worried at all. He was too involved in reading those reports. His eyes were glued to the pages until Dr. Franklin interrupted us.

"Come in, Detective Zoolu. Is this the friend you were talking about during our last visit?" asked Dr. Franklin, as we stood up to greet him.

"Yes. This is Detective Matthew. He works for a city police department just east of here. I haven't really explained to him yet why I had him come with me."

"Why is he here today?"

"He will verify the story I told you last week. I would like you to hear his story from his own lips. You wouldn't believe me, but maybe you'll believe him. We both experienced similar events. But I'll let him tell it." I followed the doctor into his office, while Matthew stayed in the outer office. "Can I bring Detective Matthew along?"

"Why don't we leave him in the waiting room for now?" said Dr. Franklin, as he shut the door behind us. "I would like to speak with *you* right now. I would like to clear up a few things and then by all means, I'd be very interested in hearing his explanation to these so-called, mysterious events. Now please, take a seat." We sat down in our respective chairs.

I spoke up first, trying not to slur my words. "I really wanted you to hear my friend's story. Then, you might not think I'm so crazy. I know my story sounds very mysterious and unbelievable. But Doc, when you read the ballistics and analysis reports on the evidence I have uncovered and listen to Detective Matthew's eyewitness testimony, you might have a different conclusion than you had when we talked last."

"First, Detective Zoolu, let me ask you about your drinking. You haven't stopped, have you? You've been hitting the sauce pretty hard, haven't you?"

I nodded. "So what if I have? If you were suspended from your job, what would you do? What else *is* there to do? I drink to forget about my problems."

He retorted, "Why do you feel it necessary to drink so much, day after day? Do you know, you are killing yourself?" He looked down at his notebook and began writing in it.

"If I was working, I wouldn't be drinking as much, if at all?"

He looked me in the eyes and said, "I want to prescribe you medicine that will help you control your binge drinking. Then maybe your delusions will disappear."

"There you go again," I replied angrily, "calling my experience delusions. That's the reason I brought my friend with me today. He can back up my story. Please, let's bring him in here, now."

"I promise, I'll listen to his story in a minute. But I have a few more questions to ask you."

I became angry. "No. I'm not going to sit here and listen to you tell me I'm having delusions. I want Detective Matthew in here, right now. Let him tell you himself what he experienced in that area. I refuse to say another word until you agree to bring the detective in here and listen to his story."

"If you insist. I think this is utterly ridiculous. But if it will soothe your hurt feelings, then I'll agree to listen to his explanation, no matter how unbelievable it may sound. Go ahead and bring him in."

Dr. Franklin continued writing in his little notebook as I left the room to bring Detective Matthew into his office.

I returned to the waiting room and retrieved Detective Matthew. Despite his unwillingness to leave his seat or get involved, we entered the doctor's office together.

"Doc, I want you to listen to Detective Matthew's story. He'll verify that everything I've told you is true. He's my eyewitness to the mysterious phenomenon. Go ahead, Detective Matthew tell him your story," I said eagerly, sitting down to listen.

"What do you want me to tell him?" asked Matthew, giving me a dirty look.

"I want you to explain to the doctor, what happened to you when you drove out to that area and visited that mysterious town," I said, as Detective Matthew remained silent. "Do you know what you are doing to me by not telling the doctor your story? He'll think I'm really crazy if you don't speak up. Don't do this to me. You were my only hope."

"I'm sorry," Matthew said apologetically. "But we talked about this before. I don't know what to tell him? I don't think you should get me involved in your discussions with your psychiatrist,"

"Detective Matthew, John, don't do this to me," I pleaded.

"If you don't need me anymore, Doctor, I'll leave now and return to the waiting room and finish my reading," said Matthew, as he turned to leave the room.

"You have nothing you want to tell me then, Detective Matthew?" asked Dr. Franklin.

"I'm sorry to have been involved in this little discussion. Dr. Franklin, I wish I could say the words you want to hear to help Detective Zoolu get back to his job. But I don't know what you want from me? I shouldn't have been put in this situation. I'm sorry." With that said, Matthew walked out of the doctor's office and into the waiting room.

"I'm speechless," I told the doc. "Now you will really think I'm crazy. I know when I've been stabbed in the back. Not only by a good friend, but also a fellow detective. I feel like a complete imbecile, a real horse's ass. I just can't believe Detective Matthew would do that to me? I have lost all trust in that man."

"I'm sure, in time, you will forget all about this. I will forget this ever happened, if you can," promised Dr. Franklin.

"How can I forget? I had expected him to come to bat for me. But what does he do? He chickens out. I should have expected it. Well, I guess that's my own fault."

"I wouldn't say that. You're just going through a rough time right now."

"That's putting it mildly,"

"In time, you will have a different perspective on life. As I said before, I am prescribing you a medicine that will help you. But I want to forget what transpired here today. We'll start anew, next week. Same time, same place." He handed me the prescription.

"Fine. I'll see you next week at three o'clock," I replied, as I stood up, turned and left the room.

I walked past Detective Matthew without saying a word. He followed silently behind as we rode the elevator to the garage, then walked to the car. We were both silent. As we entered the car, I gave Matthew a dirty look, then drove directly to my place. I constantly shook my head in disgust and disbelief during the ride in the car.

"What did you want me to say?" asked Matthew.

"Nothing, of course. I wanted to look like an utter fool. Now that doctor really thinks I'm loony," I snapped, slapping Matthew on the arm.

"Well, it's all your fault."

"What the hell do you mean, it's my fault?" I barked, pulling the car over to the side of the road so we could argue.

"You're the one that told me not to tell anyone my story," exclaimed Matthew. "You said it, yourself. You told me I shouldn't jeopardize my job when you had already jeopardized yours. That's exactly what you said."

"I didn't mean it in *that* situation. Especially, when you knew how important that appointment was in getting my suspension lifted."

"Excuse me," snapped Matthew. "I didn't know we were going to your doctor…or why you wanted me there. I didn't know, that is, until I walked into that room and you surprised me and shoved it down my throat."

"Now the doctor thinks I'm stone nuts. He'll never lift my suspension. Not after witnessing this little episode. After this, I wouldn't be surprised if he transfers me to the nut house. I wanted him to listen to your story. Then I was going to show him the ballistics reports on the evidence I had uncovered." Getting that off my chest, I turned back onto the highway and sped away towards home.

"Do you really think he would have believed me?" asked Matthew. "He probably would have put us both in the nut house."

"He might have? But now, we'll never know? When I needed your help the most, you let me down. I really never expected that from you. I thought I could trust you completely. Now I know I was wrong."

"You *can* trust me. Look. When I entered that room, your question took me by surprise. I just froze. I'm sorry. But when I reacted to the situation, I remembered the words you said to me. That's the first thing that came to mind. You said don't jeopardize your job. If you tell anyone this story they'll think you're crazy. Those were your exact words. Just remember that."

I remained silent. We had arrived at my place. I was still quite angry with Matthew even though I knew he had only done what I had told him to do. I knew in the back of my mind it wasn't his fault. I had made a fool out of myself at the psychiatrist's office.

Now I just wanted to go in the house, drink some scotch, and forget my troubles. I walked silently up the steps to my front door. I turned to see if Matthew was following behind me. But he was walking slowly to his car.

"Detective Matthew, do you want to come in for a cup of coffee?" I shouted.

"Hell, after what just happened, I thought you didn't want to speak to me anymore," he yelled, standing next to his vehicle, twenty feet away from me.

"I really don't. But I just thought I would be polite. Give me a few days. I'll get over it."

"All right. I'll be talking to you," Matthew replied loudly as he unlocked his car door. "Hey, are you going to the Policeman's Costume Ball?"

I shook my head and replied, "I doubt it. But I don't know for sure." I turned and walked into the house and shut the door behind me.

I listened as Detective Matthew's car sped off down the road. I wondered if he would be going to the costume ball. I thought about **Matthew's** aging disease. I still hadn't mentioned it to him. But I had noticed quite a few more wrinkles on his face and his hair had turned partially white. But that thought quickly left my mind.

I went directly to the kitchen and reached for my magic bottle. I held it close to my body and waltzed into the living room and fell onto the couch. I turned on the police scanner and began pouring down shots of scotch, until I passed out.

During the next few days, I remained stone drunk while my body continued to ripen with age. But that wasn't what was worrying me. I wanted desperately to win back my job. But that seemed as hopeless as I was. I ran amok in self-pity. The booze helped numb my sorrow. By staying drunk, the days seemed to go by much quicker. Every night, during my binge, I would pass out on the couch and every night I would awaken from that same damn nightmare. It refused to go away. There was nothing I could do to shake it from my mind.

On the third day of my drinking binge, I was suddenly awakened by a call on the police scanner. The dispatcher asked for any patrol unit to help a woman in distress. A neighbor had called in a complaint about a hysterical woman, dressed up in some nutty costume, who had stopped traffic after narrowly escaping injury from a speeding car. The crazed woman was ranting and raving that her husband had disappeared right in front of her eyes.

Within a few minutes, a police unit had arrived on the scene and called it in. I listened to the police scanner and to the conversation between the officer and dispatch. The officer stated that a young woman was walking in the street, stopping traffic, while parading around in some outrageous costume. When I heard the call, I jumped out of bed and tried to stand up. It took a few minutes to get my head on straight and change my clothes.

Ten minutes after I had heard the call, hangover or not, I was out the door and heading for the address. I had to be very, very careful or I would surely lose my job, but the need to investigate this situation was more important.

When I arrived at the address, the ambulance and patrol units were already there. I pulled up behind one of the patrol cars. I could see the victim lying inside the ambulance alone while the female attendants were off to the side talking and joking with the male police officers. I walked up to the back of the ambulance to talk with the woman. She was lying down on a gurney with her eyes shut. I stepped inside the ambulance to speak with her. When she sensed my presence, she opened her eyes and was startled to see me sitting alongside of her.

I showed her my ID. "Don't be alarmed, Miss. I'm Detective Zoolu."

"I'm Mrs. Gant," said the frightened woman.

"I'm glad to meet you. I'm here to take your statement. Can you tell me what happened? You say your husband disappeared?"

"Yes. He disappeared right in front of my eyes. We were going to a costume ball tonight. And somehow, we ended up at this funny out-of-the-way town that had a little costume shop."

"Did you rent your costumes there?"

"Yes, I told you, we were going to the Policeman's Costume Ball. But we didn't plan to rent them there. It just worked out that way."

"What do you mean?"

"We were just driving along the road, when all of a sudden we were climbing up a mountain road. I still haven't figured out how we got there. I swear the mountain came out of nowhere. I didn't know we had any mountains in this state," said Mrs. Gant, seemingly very shaken and nervous.

"Why didn't you turn the car around?" I asked.

"We couldn't."

"Why not?"

"Something had control of us. Something had control of our total beings. And by the time our senses had returned, we found ourselves in this little, ghost town."

"What did you do next?"

"We went to the only place that was open. It was called the Costume Shop. We thought it was a strange coincidence that we had ended up at a different costume shop than the one we had set out for but we had no control over the situation. And we still needed to rent costumes for the Ball, so we decided to check out the costumes inside the shop."

"I presume you picked out your costumes. Is that right?" I asked her. She nodded. "Yes, I'm wearing mine."

"I see. So what happened after you had entered the costume shop?"

"My husband and I picked out our costumes, changed into them and then, as we were leaving the shop, I saw a flash of bright light and heard an explosion. That's when I saw my husband blow up right in front of my eyes." She began crying hysterically.

"Was he walking out the front door when you saw the flash of light and heard the explosion?" I asked, already knowing the answer.

"Yes. I think so," she whined. "I mean, one second he was there and the next second, he wasn't."

"What happened to you?"

"I was thrown to the floor of the shop," cried Mrs. Gant, "and I must have passed out because the next thing I knew, I was in the middle of a busy highway, dodging speeding vehicles and still wearing the costume that I had rented. I don't know how I ended up in the middle of a highway, and I can't remember leaving the costume shop. My mind's a complete blank."

"You're not that bad. You remembered some things. Do you know what caused the explosion?"

"Yes I do. Believe it or not, I saw a World War II, German Panzer tank fire and hit my husband with enough force that his body flew in a million tiny parts. Just for an instant, I thought he had stepped smack dab in the middle of a war."

"Why do you say that?"

"I saw hundreds of German soldiers following behind the tanks. When one of them saw my husband dressed in his American officer's uniform, he stopped, sighted his weapon at him and fired at the same time as the tank. I didn't see my husband again after that."

"Why not?"

"That blast knocked me down and slammed the door shut. And like I said, the next thing I remember I was in the middle of the street dodging traffic still wearing my costume." She pulled down the blanket that covered her body and showed me her witches costume.

"How many minutes passed from the first flash of bright light to the death of your husband?" I asked, as I covered her with the blanket.

"I'm sure it was a matter of seconds. But it seemed like hours. And I saw two flashes of light, not just one."

"Two? Why two?"

"The first occurred when my husband stepped outside and the second, when the tank fired its cannon. The blow from that weapon killed my husband and it knocked me to the floor."

"When the door slammed shut and you were thrown to the floor, did you get up and open the door to look outside again?"

"No. I don't think so," said Mrs. Gant, rubbing her puffy eyes. "I just remember getting knocked to the floor, and when I woke up, I was standing in the street."

The ambulance attendants ended their conversation with the police officers, so I quickly jumped out of the ambulance.

"Thank you, Mrs. Gant for the interview. I must be going now," I said, as I walked back to my car without being noticed by the police officers.

I was very angry that I had to act this way. I had to sneak around like a thief in the night. I was still feeling the results from my weeklong drinking binge and looked as if I had died and then, dug myself out of my grave. I looked like hell. But I didn't care. I wanted my job back. I wanted to complete my investigation and find out what had happened to my partner, Detective Webber.

I decided to drive to the station to plead my case. I wanted to beg Captain Bird to give me another chance and lift my suspension. I desperately wanted my job back. I would get down on my hands and knees and beg him if I had to. I didn't care. I was in no mood to take "no" for an answer. So I drove directly to the police station. I quickly parked the car and walked directly into Captain Bird's office.

"What the hell are you doing, Zoolu, barging into my office like this? What has gotten into you? My god man, look at you. You are a very sick individual. Have you been on a drinking binge?" barked Captain Bird, as he walked past me and shut his office door. "What in god's name are you doing here?"

"I'm sorry, sir. But I'm going out of my mind with nothing to do. I've uncovered some startling new evidence on my partner's disappearance. I want another chance to investigate his case," I pleaded, as I leaned against his desk so I wouldn't fall down.

"Zoolu, you are on suspension," snarled Captain Bird, as he walked back to his desk and sat down in his chair. "You are supposed to be working on getting clean and sober. But instead, you go on a drinking binge. And you smell like a skid row bum. I shouldn't allow you in my office until you change your lifestyle. I don't know when you collected this new evidence, but if I find out that you have been investigating your partner's disappearance while you were on suspension, I'll have you fired. Believe me. I will."

"Please, sir. I didn't come here to get you upset or angry. But, I will do anything you want so I can get back to work. Please Captain, lift my suspension."

"Quite whining. You're making yourself look like a jackass. The only work I want you to be doing is getting sober. I don't want to see your face again until you are one hundred percent clean and sober. Do you hear me Detective Zoolu? Is that clear?"

"Yes sir. But isn't there anything I can do now to get my job back? I'm so close to finding the answers to my partner's disappearance that I'm confident that the case will be solved as soon as I can get back on it."

"Don't you listen? I told you to go home and clean up your act. You'll be lucky if you're back to work in three months. You're lucky I don't fire you on the spot for this ridiculous outburst."

"Captain Bird, I beg you, sir. Lift my suspension. I can't go on like this," I pleaded, as I leaned on his desk to confront him face to face. "If you won't lift my suspension, then I'll have to take matters into my own hands."

"And just what do you mean by that? I hope you're not threatening me," snapped Captain Bird, his face coming within an inch of mine.

"No, sir. It's not a threat. It's a promise. All I've done is to tell the truth and I'm condemned and belittled for it. You and the psychiatrist have called me delusional."

"I did not call you delusional."

"Well, I will prove to you sooner or later that I am not delusional and I will have the evidence to back up my claims. I'll prove that the 'Legend of Hollow Pass' is true."

"Are you serious?"

"I had hoped Detective Matthew would have backed up my story, but I had put too much trust into people. It was my own fault. I should have known better. But I promise you that I will one day find the proof that I need to get my respect and good name back. You have made me the laughing stock of this department," I shouted, walking towards the door.

"You **are** delusional" bellowed Captain Bird. "You brought all this trouble on yourself. If you remember, nobody forced you to get drunk and get arrested for drunk driving."

"Sir, I know I'm partially to blame for my behavior," I told him, opening the door to leave, "but what I've told you about the phenomenon I experienced was the complete truth. Do you honestly think I would tell a crazy story like that if it wasn't the truth?"

"I'm not going to argue with you about this subject. This conversation is finished. I want you to go home and get control of your addiction."

"When can I return to work?"

"I am going to keep in close touch with your psychiatrist. Then, when I'm satisfied that you are a changed man and you are clean and sober and plan to stay that way, then and only then, will I let you return to work. But now, leave my office." Bird pointed to the open door.

"Captain. Before I leave, I was just wondering if you were going to the Policeman's Costume Ball tonight.

"I have to. I'm the Master of Ceremony. I won last year's best costume contest and the winner was to be this year's Master of Ceremony. Why? Are you going?"

"I don't know? If my plans work out, I'll be there. If not, I may not see you for a long while," I said, as I walked out of his office.

Nearly all the detectives and officers had listened to my conversation with Captain Bird. They watched as I walked out of the station in disgust. Just as I was opening my car door, Detective Matthew came running up to me.

"I'm glad I caught you. I have been calling you all week long, but you never answered your phone," said Matthew, acting as though nothing had happened between us. "I wanted to know if you were going to the Policeman's Costume Ball tonight. If you were, do you want some company?"

"I plan on it. But I don't know if I will make it? I have some work to do first before I can go."

"What do you have to do?"

"I'm going to prove my testimony was truthful. I'm not going to sit at home and deteriorate. I'm going to take matters into my own hands," I said, as I jumped into my car and gunned the engine.

"Hey, where are you going? Let me come with you," yelled Matthew, as he watched me drive away.

Looking into my rear-view mirror, I saw Detective Matthew jump into his vehicle and give chase. He was following some distance behind my vehicle. I decided to drive out to that town and try out my theory. If it worked, great. If it didn't, well I would be out of a job. But I was out of a job anyway. So what did it matter?

But I was adamant to win back the respect of my peers at the station. I had become the laughing stock of my department and refused to be the butt of their jokes. I finally had decided to take matters into my own hands. I was going to rent a costume from that shop to wear to tonight's ball. I wanted to put matters to rest, once and for all. I was going to prove or disprove my theory.

I would have liked for Detective Matthew to be my eyewitness, but I had trusted him once and he turned his back on me. I wasn't about to give him a second chance to destroy me. I raced to the mysterious town. In my rear-view mirror, I could see Matthew's car nearly a quarter mile behind me. I pushed the accelerator to the floor. I wanted to further the distance between us. Nearly two hours later, Matthew's car had fallen so far behind that I couldn't see it in my rear-view mirror anymore. I wasn't sure if he was following me or not? I really didn't care, either.

Just then the mountain appeared out of nowhere. I began driving up that steep incline, heading towards that crazy town. The second my car began climbing up that steep mountain road, the weather turned from a beautiful, dry, sunny day to just the opposite. It was no different than before. The dark, black clouds turned into a thick, foggy mist the farther up I climbed the narrow, winding mountain road. The wind continued to push the car all over the road. Thankfully, there weren't any other cars on the road in the area. By the time I had reached the top of the mountain, the spirit or entities had once again control of my entire being and my vehicle.

The wind began to push the car down the winding mountain road faster and faster. I could do nothing about it. It was the same each time I had visited this strange area. But this time I was going to get the positive evidence that I needed to solve my investigation to my partner's disappearance. However, I had to do it on my own. Nobody would believe my circumstantial evidence or my word. Now I was going to make them eat their words. I was going to prove once and for all that I had been telling the truth all along.

First, I needed to get down this mysterious mountain alive. The last few hundred feet traveling down that mountain road the wind and foul weather pushed my vehicle at a tremendous speed. Finally, I found myself at the bottom of the canyon. I felt a slight shiver travel through my body, but at least now I had full control of my faculties and my vehicle. I pushed the accelerator to the floor and headed for the costume shop and that strange town.

I looked into my rear-view mirror for Matthew's vehicle but it was nowhere to be seen. I must have been farther ahead than I thought; either that, or he had turned back and stopped following me.

While driving towards the town, I noticed two figures a few hundred feet ahead of me. It looked like the huge Indian man and the boy. I pushed the accelerator to the floor hoping to catch up to them. I wanted to ask them some questions, especially that boy. I had hoped he could tell me what the words, "*Go Thru Door*" meant? Those were the words that kept coming to me in my nightmares. But for some odd reason, I was never able to catch up to them. When I got within ten feet of the two figures, they would disappear before my eyes. By the time I had finished rubbing my eyes and wondering if they were a mirage or not, I had arrived at the costume shop.

Before I entered the shop, I sat in my car and wrote a letter, just in case something went wrong with my theory and I didn't return. I wanted the truth to be heard. I wasn't about to try out my theory without leaving an explanation for my actions. I placed the note in a large envelope, along with my journal about my investigation and this mysterious town, and included the analysis reports of the costume and the ballistics' report on the three spent bullet fragments. I also placed the bullets into the envelope then sealed it shut. But the costume was at my place. I put the envelope into my jacket pocket and walked into the costume shop. Just as I entered, I turned on a miniature tape recorder I had hidden in my jacket pocket to record the conversation for future reference and would use it as evidence if my plan worked out. If it didn't. Oh, well.

Jackson Billing, the hunchbacked, old man was sitting behind his counter, as though he had been waiting for me all along.

"Well, well. Look who's back," said the bug-eyed, old man, as he stared at me through his thick, wire-rimmed glasses.

"Yeah. But this time, I come as a customer. I need to rent one of your costumes for tonight's Costume Ball. Do you mind if I rent one?" I asked, looking into his beady, magnified eyes for his reaction.

"Not at all. I was waiting for you. Go ahead. Pick out a nice one."

"When are you going to give up your secrets to this place and free the spirits? When will the gods be satisfied with their retribution? Or is it revenge they want?"

"I am only the caretaker to this place. The answers you want are not within me, but within you. You will find the answer, sooner than you know."

"Well, Mr. Billing. Which costume do you suggest I wear to tonight's costume ball?" I asked, as I looked through rack after rack of costumes.

"I'm sure, you'll find the one you like."

Just as he said that, my eyes caught the attention of an old coonskin hat and a fringed, leather outfit. It was the costume of Davey Crockett, king of the wild frontier. As I grabbed the costume from the rack and started walking towards the back to the little changing room, the shop's front door burst open. I turned to see who it was. Low and behold, it was Detective Matthew.

"Am I too late?" yelled Detective Matthew, red faced and out of breath, as he stood in the shop's open doorway.

"Too late for what, Detective Matthew?" I asked, as I turned to speak with him.

"What are you doing?" he asked, as he shut the door behind him.

"What does it look like? I'm trying on a costume," I replied, as I entered the little changing room.

"Why? Are you going to the Policeman's Costume Ball tonight?" asked Matthew.

"I guess I am if I'm going to rent a costume? Boy, are you a smart one."

"Well, if you don't mind, I'll rent one too and we can go to the ball together. If that's all right with you?" asked Matthew, as he stood nearby and waited for me to come out of the changing room.

"You do what you want," I snapped, as I changed into my costume. "Don't ask me for anything. You stabbed me in the back. Remember?"

"Please, don't hold that against me. I only did what you told me to do."

While I was busy changing into my Davey Crockett costume, Detective Matthew was searching for one. He was trying to get back into my good graces. But that wasn't important to me anymore. The only important thing now was to prove my theory that the "Legend of Hollow Pass" was really true. Now, I even had an eyewitness to my actions. I was in a no-lose situation. If my theory worked, I would win. And if something went wrong, I still won, because I had an eyewitness to report the news. But I planned on nothing going wrong. I knew what I had to do.

When I came out of that changing room wearing my costume, Detective Matthew had finally picked out one and began walking to the dressing room. He had chosen the Wild Bill Hickock costume. It looked like the real clothes that Wild Bill had worn the day he had been assassinated: It had a wide, brimmed hat, and double ivory handled forty-five caliber pistols, down to the spurs on his boots.

Detective Matthew walked into the room to change into his costume while I waited near the counter. I didn't plan on waiting for him though. He was going to be my witness. I discreetly placed the envelope with my letter, journal, photocopies, recorder and other evidence, in Detective

Matthew's jacket pocket as it was hanging up while he was changing into his costume. Just as he was coming out of the changing room, I decided to try out my theory.

Just as I stepped through the open door of the costume shop, I could hear Detective Matthew as he tried to call me back. I'm sure he saw a bright, flash of light and then saw me die at the siege of the Alamo. Now it would be up to him to carry on with the investigation of this mysterious town and its strange costume shop. When he reads the letter and journal, and listens to the tape recording, he will understand what he has to do in the future. Now, **he** will be the one to bare the burden of this mysterious area. This phenomenon of the gods. And the Legend of Hollow Pass.

.

The End...Or is it?

P.S. A letter was taped to the inside of the journal from a Detective Matthew explaining the last few pages of the journal. It seems Matthew had found a miniature cassette recording from a recorder in Zoolu's jacket pocket that he had left behind in the costume shop before disappearing, which Zoolu had used to record the conversations of Billing, Matthew and himself, including his explanation of what he thought would happen as he went through the door dressed in his costume; and using this information Matthew finished the last few pages of the journal in Zoolu's own words before leaving it on my doorstep.

Signed,
Bobby Legend
(Investigative reporter)

EPILOGUE

Detective Zoolu has passed through the vortex. Now it's up to Detective Matthew to investigate this matter. Will he save Zoolu or is he gone forever? You will have to read Costume Shop II to find out what happens next.